Baby's
GOT BITE
a *Take It Like a Vamp* novel

CANDACE HAVENS

Entangled Publishing, LLC
2614 South Timberline Road
Suite 109
Fort Collins, CO 80525
Visit our website at www.entangledpublishing.com.

Covet is an imprint of Entangled Publishing, LLC.

Edited by Stephen Morgan & Ava Jae
Cover design by Curtis Svehlak
Cover art from Shutterstock

Manufactured in the United States of America

First Edition July 2015

*To Heather Riccio, Meredith Johnson and Katie Clapsadl,
and the rest of Linc's fans, this book is for you!*

Chapter One

Who gets married on a private island to a Greek Billionaire?

Bennett stood to the left of her best friend Casey, who was doing exactly that—getting married—under a flowered archway in front of the bluest ocean she'd ever seen.

Sure people fell in love all the time, but getting married? Committing yourself to one person for a really long time? That wasn't Bennett's thing.

"I do," Casey said, repeating the words Nick, her groom, had said.

It was pretty much a done deal now. No backing out. One glance at Casey and Nick was all it took to see that they were firmly nestled in their fairy-tale ending. It wasn't like Bennett wasn't happy for them. She was. Casey and Nick, they were an odd match, an artist and a billionaire, but were perfect for one another.

Bennett had tried to find the same thing herself, but it never worked. A relationship meant giving up the autonomy that kept her safe. It just went to show her that even if Happily Ever After existed, it was only possible for other people. Not her.

Casey turned to face her and take the bridal bouquet Bennett had been holding during the ceremony. Her friend was radiant.

"For a married chick, you're kind of beautiful," she said as she handed her the flowers and then kissed her cheek.

Casey sniffed — always so emotional, that one. "You don't look so bad yourself. Now I just have to make it down the aisle in these heels."

Once the bride and groom had gone halfway down, Linc, Nick's best friend and best man, stepped up and offered his arm.

God, he's gorgeous.

Tall, with those lean muscles of an athlete, he had a presence. But she would never tell him that.

"Time to move, lass," he said with that accent and deep, gravelly tone. Jesus, did shivers just go down her spine?

Oh, hell no.

"I'm not an idiot," she said. "I know what happens next."

Fine, so that was totally bitchy, but there was something about him that rubbed her the wrong way — even if she couldn't stop fantasizing about him rubbing her the *right* way. Guys like him felt like they owned the world, and it just bugged her.

He chuckled.

That pissed her off even more.

And he was warm. Maybe it was the Mediterranean sun, but she could have sworn he was twenty degrees hotter.

Halfway down the aisle, it happened. Her high heel

punctured the white runner, the shoe came off, she fell forward, and the only thing keeping her from doing a face-plant were the arms wrapped tightly around her.

Linc's arms.

Crap. His skin against hers made her feel like she was going to burst into flames.

He swooped her up like they were coming out of a dip during a dance, and then he righted her.

"Are you all right?" His beautiful eyes were full of concern.

Dammit. Why did he have to be so handsome? Why?

"Yes," she said, hating that she sounded so terse. But she couldn't help herself.

Earlier, Linc had seen her naked. He'd been in the dressing room helping Casey with last minute stuff. Bennett, who was running late, had rushed in and without thinking, stripped to her bra and her panties.

That was the first time they met.

And now she'd fallen into his arms.

Yep. She was a dork.

I need a drink.

She took off the other shoe, grabbed the one stuck to the runner, and did the mature thing.

She stomped away.

A girl could only handle so much mortification in one day.

One wedding ceremony, two tequila shots, and God knew how much champagne later, Bennett felt comfortably numb to her loneliness.

Casey and Nick walked hand in hand onto the empty floor and began to dance. Bennett was thrilled to see her friend so happy, but a small part of her—a sad, pathetic part—was jealous. She would never have this.

Not that she wanted it.

There was no way she'd be able to share her life with one guy. She'd tried, and it ended the same way every time. Things started off passionate. Exciting. But then consuming to the point that she felt confined.

She couldn't let that happen ever again.

As far as guys were concerned, from this point on, they were good for only one thing.

And damn, I could use that one thing.

When Casey and Nick finished their dance, the band played a more upbeat musical number, a signal that the rest of the wedding guests should feel free to dance, too.

Fun. This was what she needed. She'd go find a man and shake her groove thing. Tempt him. Seduce him. Then she could scratch this itch and go back to life as usual. Alone, but safe.

As soon as this song was over. Or maybe the next one.

Okay, maybe this solo sex goddess role wasn't as easy she thought.

First things first. Pick a guy to scratch this itch. Someone safe. Someone definitely not named Linc.

She caught sight of Mason, Nick's top security dude. He'd been nice to her the few times they'd chatted while helping with the wedding setup. She'd never felt particularly attracted to him, and maybe that would be a good thing tonight. She could close her eyes and think of…

Linc?

No. No. No.

She straightened her shoulders and walked—well, really, there was a bit of weaving around at that point; she might have had more tequila than she remembered—to Mason and tapped him on the shoulder. He was watching the festivities from near where the band played.

"Hey, are you working, or will the boss man let you dance with me?"

Did that sound desperate? Maybe. But stupid, sex-on-a-stick Linc had left her that way.

Mason was a hulk of a man, not fat, but wide. And tall. Kind of like a big Redwood, with the face of an angel. Perfect for a guy in the security business. A lot of Nick's people and friends were kind of perfect like that.

"Sorry, Mason. This dance is mine."

Her muddled mind didn't make sense of what she'd heard until *he* was in front of her.

"What kind of bullshit is this?" she asked, trying not to gasp as Linc slid one hand along her waist and took her hand with the other.

"I want to know why you dislike me." He pulled her into his embrace. "And I'm not letting go until you tell me the truth."

She snorted. "I don't dislike you. I just don't like what you stand for."

Crap, would her mouth never stop?

"And what, exactly, is that?"

They were moving as one, and she had no idea how. She was too tipsy to keep up, but they were making their way across the floor. God, the way his hands brushed against her hips and the small of her back, the outline of his biceps against his almost too tight button up shirt…

"Rich. Privileged. You can have any woman you want. You live a life in the tabloids, and you don't seem to care."

"And you believe everything you read."

"Well, pictures don't lie. Do you deny you have a different woman on your arm every time you go out?"

"And variety is a bad thing?"

She didn't have an answer for that. How could she judge him for the very same thing she did?

"This is a bad idea," she said.

"Is it such a chore to dance with me?"

What was she supposed to say to that? It wasn't a chore. It was driving her insane.

But come on. It wasn't just that he was a friend of Casey's. That would be complicated enough. That whole variety thing made her nervous. Not that she cared about comparing herself with other women, but she'd been mortified enough earlier when she was nearly naked in front of him.

Adding drunken sex to the mix—she'd have to move to another country.

No. That was *not* going to happen. He was the absolute last guy she was going to sleep with tonight.

Better to let him down quick and easy.

She shrugged. "You're hot. I guess you have that going for you. But you're kind of bossy and really not my type."

"And what is your type?" His voice was low, almost like a growl.

"Well, generally I go for the narcissistic asshole who doesn't care what I want, but tonight I figured I'd go for a guy who knows how to put someone else's needs above his own."

Oh. My. God. Shut the fuck up.

Well, damage done. He'd be mad, but at least he'd leave her alone.

He chuckled. "Then I'd say I'm most definitely your type."

Wait…what?

As he pulled her closer, she could have sworn he sucked in a breath. Her nipples pressed against his chest. They were so hard and tight, every movement was like an erotic caress. Warmth spread through her body.

"By my type, obviously you mean…"

Please don't say narcissistic asshole. Please. Please. Please.

He leaned in so close that his breath tickled her ear. "I mean, I know how to put a woman's needs above mine. *And* I'm a narcissistic asshole."

That made her laugh. "At least you're honest about it."

He laughed, too. "I'm offering tonight. Nothing else. If that's what you want."

A shiver slid through her body, and her face heated.

Is it getting hotter out here? She resisted the urge to fan herself.

He blinked. How did a guy have lashes that long? Why was he looking at her like he was ready to eat her up?

No. No. Bad idea.

His thumb rubbed across the back of her hand.

Holy hell.

Okay, her body insisted she go through with taking to bed the one guy she'd decided was off-limits. But hold on. Hadn't he said he was only offering tonight? Wasn't that what she was looking for?

Maybe this situation was perfect. Exactly what she

needed—the assurance that whatever happened, there was no chance of things spiraling out of control tomorrow.

"I could be persuaded," she said.

"Yeah?"

"Depends on your answer to one very important question."

"Ask anything you want," he whispered in her ear.

A tingling sensation hummed through her body. She shifted her hips closer to him, and his hard length pressed against her leg.

Holy hell.

"Could you take me back to your room and fuck my brains out?"

• • •

What did she just say?

Linc's cock tightened, and he nearly stomped on her toes when he missed a step. He'd been watching the ethereal beauty most of the day and into the night. The way she moved, laughed, and even the way she gave him shit intrigued him.

And she was tough. Just before the reception, he'd over-heard her tell Nick that if he ever hurt Casey, she'd cut him. Then she'd smiled, as if her threat was a normal thing to say among friends.

Crazy? Perhaps, but she was his kind of crazy. He'd been known to cross the line, too, when it came to protecting the people he cared about.

And more, she wasn't looking for anything beyond the night, which was perfect for him. He couldn't allow himself to get caught up in anything—let alone a relationship—that took him away from his duties. The world might see him as the head of a fashion empire, but his real job was protecting those closest to him. He'd let down his family years ago, and he would never let that happen again.

Bennett chuckled as she stumbled and fell against him.

"Are you drunk?" he asked.

No way would he take advantage of Casey's best friend—or anyone else, for that matter. But he'd known Nick two hundred years, and there was no way he'd let a drunk woman come between them.

But holy crap. The feeling of her body against his. He'd been hard all day, just thinking about how delicious she would taste as he licked her neck, her breasts, and then went lower…

"Just a little tipsy, thanks," she said. "But I'm also horny. Besides, I know what I'm doing. So if you can't get it up for me, no worries. I can try elsewhere. I just need someone with a dick. Not super picky tonight."

Something dark and possessive grew within him, surprising him, and maybe freaking him out just a little. But the idea of someone else touching her—that wasn't going to happen.

"Such a romantic," he growled.

She laughed. "Look, it's a wedding. People fuck at weddings, right? So if you're not interested, let's move it along." She glanced at the band. "Isn't this song almost over?"

No. He wouldn't let her go off and find some obliging idiot to fuck. When he'd first brought her into his arms for this dance, he'd seen something haunting in her eyes that sparked every protective instinct he had. She'd been hurt before. Badly. He wouldn't let her get hurt again tonight just because she was looking for a wild time.

If that meant he had to drop his guard and give in to his own desire so he could service hers?

"Fine."

"Fine?"

Maybe, even if just for the night, he could put a little light back in her eyes.

He pulled her close again. "If you want someone to fuck, I'll help you."

She giggled.

"What's so funny?" He guided her off the dance floor and toward the back of the mansion, where his suite was.

"Promise me one thing," she said.

He chuckled. "Okay."

"You can't tell anyone. All right? I mean...Casey would flip. And I don't want to answer a lot of questions. So pinky swear, you'll never tell anyone we did this."

"Casey would have my head, and probably some other parts I like attached to my body. Your secret is safe with me."

He pushed open the door to his suite, and once it was closed, he shoved her against it.

And then he whispered against her ear, "I swear."

She trembled under his hands. Excellent.

"Tell me what you want," he said as he pushed an errant hair behind her ear.

She fluttered those long dark lashes up at him and smiled. "I like it rough," she whispered.

Fuck, he was going to come in his pants if she didn't stop, because everything she was saying let him know she was exactly his type. Nothing got him hotter than a woman who trusted him to keep her safe no matter how wild things got in the bedroom.

The beast in him roared, and a haze of need enveloped him. He had to get inside her.

He held her arms above her head before nibbling on her ear. "So do I. And just so we're clear: one night of fucking, and we're done."

She lifted her leg and wrapped it around his waist. When she pressed her heat against his rock hard cock, he almost came undone.

He pushed the beast down. They had one night, and he would savor every second of it.

"One and done." She ground her heat against his cock. "Now stop talking and give me what I want."

Chapter Two

Ten weeks later

"Does my ass look huge in these jeans?" Bennett turned around in the dressing room's three-way mirror. She'd always been straight as a board. But her jeans no longer fit, and now she was trying to find a pair that didn't make her feel like her spleen and liver might be severed.

Where the hell had these curves come from?

Casey didn't even look up from her phone. "I hate it when skinny people talk about being fat. You can wear anything."

"Just look up."

Her friend did as asked…and smiled. "About time you finally grew up and got an ass and some hips."

"Casey! Come on. I'm freaking out here. What's happening to me?"

Her friend stood, put one hand under her chin, and gave

Bennett a once over. "There's no delicate way to say this, but are you hitting the Chunky Monkey a little hard?"

"No," Bennett said. "I don't even like ice cream."

"No reason to get so snippy. Maybe you're just on your period. God knows I gain like five pounds whenever mine comes."

Period? Bennett's stomach sank to her toes as she choked down a gasp. She'd been so busy with work, she hadn't thought about that. When *was* the last time she had her period? She counted on her fingers.

Five weeks... Six weeks... Nine weeks...

Too long. It'd been too long. "Shit. Shit. Shit."

"What?" Casey dumped her phone into her giant purse.

Bennett's head felt light and fuzzy as stars spotted her vision. She sat on the floor before she could pass out. "This is a size bigger than I normally wear, and it's still tight."

Casey shrugged. "Hell, I can go up a size overnight. And you're going from a zero to a two. It's not really a travesty."

Bennett's head dropped between her knees, and she forced herself to take deep breaths. "Oh God."

Casey grabbed her hand and squeezed. "Honey, I'm sorry. You're beautiful and still super skinny. I was just giving you a hard time."

How could it have been so long? Maybe she'd miscounted. Or maybe it was just a fluke. Or maybe...

She counted back again. Shortly before Casey's wedding. Just in time for her to go after that hunk on a stick fashion designer—

No. It couldn't be.

"It's not that." Her voice was hoarse with unshed tears. "Ten weeks."

"Ten weeks what?" Casey knelt beside her.

"Since my period."

"Oh. Ohhh. Wow. Okay. Well, that is, um... So you're late. That can be caused by a lot of things. So can the weight gain. And you told me it's been forever since you've been with a guy."

Except for that one time.

Crap. Crap. Crap.

"You know how I thought I had the flu last week?" she croaked.

"But you got over it," Casey said hopefully. "You don't get over morning sickness that fast. And the flu can also cause your body to go out of whack. Any kind of sickness can."

Her body was definitely out of whack, but could it be so simple? Never in her life had she wanted so much to just be sick.

She shrugged, her head still down. "But I'm not really over it. I've been sticking with soup and crackers for the last eight days, because it's the only thing that sounds good. That's why I was surprised my jeans were so tight."

"Okay, but you haven't been with a guy in ages, so unless this is immaculate conception..."

Bennett winced and picked at her fraying socks. Maybe soup and crackers for breakfast wasn't as safe as she thought.

"Oh God. Look at me," Casey ordered. "Bennett, what are you not telling me?"

She sighed. "At the wedding..."

"At the wedding?"

"There was this guy..."

"No," Casey said. "You didn't... Did you?"

Bennett peeked up at Casey. She didn't have to say it. The not-so-celibate truth was written all over her face.

"Well, that does it," Casey said. "We aren't going to find any answers sitting on the floor of this dressing room. Get out of those jeans. We're going to the drug store."

Forty-five minutes later they were at Casey and Nick's penthouse apartment, staring at six pink sticks lined up on the bathroom counter.

All of them positive.

Not for nothing, but she was still waiting to see what the seventh stick revealed.

Come on. Give me just a little hope...

"I'm going to make a terrible mother," Bennett whispered. "Remember that time we were doing that campaign for the organic baby food company? Those kids howled every time I came near them."

"It's different when it's yours." Casey pulled her into the living room and onto the couch. "At least that's what people say."

Bennett stared out the floor to ceiling windows. God. How could she have been so stupid? One stinking night. *One.* And she could have sworn they'd used a condom. They'd been buzzed and excited about getting a taste of each other, but she'd never have a one-night stand without one...

"Thanks for not asking questions right now," Bennett said. "I promise I'll tell you everything, but I need a day or two to figure things out."

She'd never planned on kids. Ever. It hurt her to her

core knowing her parents had split before she'd been born. Whenever she asked about her dad, her mother said he didn't exist. Even before the cancer took her, she refused to give Bennett his name. Eventually, Bennett had stopped caring.

As far as she was concerned, she owed her parents a big thank you for splitting up. They'd taught her she could take care of herself. Hell, that she *had* to take care of herself. Asking someone else to take on a portion of that responsibility was just asking to be let down.

But this was something else.

She'd promised herself long ago she'd never put her own kids through the kind of torment she'd gone through. That was easy to say when she was childless. But now? How the hell was she supposed to live up to that promise when—assuming this last pregnancy test didn't give her a sliver of hope—she was already ten weeks pregnant?

A baby. What the fuck was she going to do with a baby?

Casey peeked at the seventh stick. "Positive."

Bennett groaned and covered her face with her hands. This was a nightmare. It couldn't be true. It just couldn't. "What am I going to do?"

Her friend hugged her. "I'm here for you. No matter what. We're going to deal with this together. I texted my doc, Jacinda. She's amazing. And I mean it, from here on out, you aren't alone. Though I do think you might want to tell the dad."

Bennett blew out a breath. Casey would freak out if she knew who the father was.

"It was just a one-night stand. I won't force him to be a father to some kid he wasn't planning."

"You think that's what happened with your dad?"

"I don't know. I mean, Mom never talked about it, but the situation had to be pretty bad for her to leave him before I was born."

"Aw, honey. Is that the story with this guy? He can't be that bad if he made it through that impenetrable armor you put up whenever I've tried to set you up with someone."

Okay yeah, Linc had irritated the hell out of her before she'd pulled down her panties for him. But did that mean he didn't deserve to know about the baby? Her mom may have never even given Bennett's father the option to be in his child's life. She couldn't do the same thing to Linc.

She saw two likely outcomes.

One, he'd want nothing to do with her. Bad, but she'd deal with it.

Two, he'd want to stick around and help. Good, right? Except that was maybe worse. As much as the idea intrigued her, she'd been down that road, being with a guy who wanted to be there for her but didn't know when to back off. It only took a couple of weeks before a man doting on her began to feel suffocating.

"I'm going to be sick."

"Do you want to get the bucket, or can you make it to the toilet?" Casey moved to help her up.

"No, not that kind of sick. Just overwhelmed. I don't know what the hell to do."

But that wasn't really true. She knew what she *should* do—she needed to tell Linc. At least make him a part of the conversation.

"Can I take a rain check on the pizza you offered?" she asked. "I need to go talk to…you know who."

"Your mystery lover? Okay. Do you want me to come?"

Eek. If Casey came, she'd see Linc. Should she tell her friend everything up front? Get all the secrets out before they had a chance to explode?

No. Not until she talked to Linc.

"I need to go alone."

"Okay. But I mean it, Ben. We're in this together. You text me, and I'll be right over." She squeezed her friend's arm. "You're going to be fine."

Bennett forced a small smile, but she wasn't so convinced.

He's going to hate me.

• • •

"I don't like the way these shorts look, Linc. You can't make me wear them."

Supermodels were a necessary evil in his business, but Marina Kolov was Lucifer incarnate. A six-month stay in rehab for coke addiction had done nothing for her attitude. As much as he loved women—and hell, he loved them more than anything—Marina drove him up the road to crazy.

"Luv, that arse of yours is God's gift to men. You know it. I know it. My clothes make it look like your ass won the lottery. Give us a turn."

She stuck her lips out in a pout, but there was approval in her eyes as she turned in the three-way mirror.

Marina might be beautiful, but she didn't compare to a certain raven-haired beauty plaguing his dreams.

"What shirt do you want on, Marina?" His assistant, Claire, asked with a bored sigh.

He couldn't blame her. This had to be one of the longest

shoots in history, even though they'd only been at it for three hours. Marina did that to people.

"No shirt. Marina, I want the pout. Cross your arms, hands on your breasts. Got it?" She rolled her eyes, but she was an exhibitionist, so he knew she couldn't care less if she was bare-chested.

His phone rang, and Nick's name crawled across the screen.

Linc answered the call. "What's up?"

"The girls are up to something." Nick sounded panicked.

Linc smiled. His brother-in-arms was paranoid when it came to a certain woman in his life.

"They're always up to something," Linc said as he nodded to the photographer trying to get his attention. The model's short shorts were riding up her arse. Perfect. Sex sold. No one knew that better than he did.

Marina glanced over her shoulder and pouted. Yep. She might be a demon, but she would sell the hell out of his new clothing line.

"Not like this," Nick said. "Casey kicked the security team out of the penthouse."

Linc chuckled. He pointed to the long button-down shirt he'd designed to go over one of the shorter skirts. Claire picked it up along with the skirt and motioned for Marina to follow her.

"Are you laughing?"

"Don't worry," Linc said. "No one can get in this fortress. We have guards everywhere. And I'm five floors down in the photography studio. They'll be fine."

"I guess. But I haven't seen her since this morning. She was asleep when I left. My plane just landed, and she's not even returning my texts."

And there it was. Nick had it bad for Casey. He couldn't blame the vampire. She was beyond awesome—beautiful, funny, and smart. The whole package. She and Nick had been friends who finally figured out they were meant for eternity.

In a lot of ways, he envied them. But he wasn't a long-term kind of guy. That sort of thing wasn't in the cards for him. Nick was head of the Supernatural Council, and Linc was his second-in-command. Between Linc's duties to the council, helping to run the army of security that protected them, and his own business, he didn't have time for anything that lasted longer than a single night.

He wouldn't let anyone get hurt on his watch, which meant he couldn't afford to get distracted by falling in love—even lust—with anyone.

Still, he was glad his friends had found one another.

Casey's friend Bennett flashed through his brain. She was the whole package in a different way. Oh, she had the smart and beautiful thing down, but he didn't like that he couldn't get her out of his head.

Not going there.

"My guess is once she knows you're in the building, she won't keep you waiting for long. Hey, one of the buyers gave me tickets for one of the corporate boxes at the Cowboys' game on Sunday. Want to come?"

"Let me check with the wife, but yes."

Linc didn't call Nick out, but damn, Casey had him whipped bad.

"Mason said they had a bunch of bags from CVS in the limo. Bennett had the flu last week. Do you think Casey is sick?"

"So what if she is? She'll get better."

Nick growled. "I'm going home. This is bullshit. I need to know if she's okay."

Linc let out a silent sigh when he heard Nick mention Bennett. What he'd give to have just one more night with her...

No. No. No.

They'd agreed nothing would happen beyond that one night. For everyone's good.

"Oh, hold on," Nick said. "Casey says it's okay for me to go home. Just got a text."

"There ya go. Let me know about the game."

Linc ended the call, then looked at the shots on the computer and pointed out a few he liked to the photographer.

He rubbed his beard when Marina returned. Something wasn't quite right. Her torso was longer than the model he'd used for the fitting. The bottom of the shirt hit the skirt at the wrong angle.

"Hold up." Linc unbuttoned the bottom of the shirt and tied it into a bow at mid-waist. He rested his hands on Marina's hips to measure that the sides of the shirt were even. "There you are, love."

"Linc, someone is here to see you," Claire said.

He turned just in time to see Bennett. She shook her head, worry etched on her face. But before he could reach her, she took off toward the hallway. Maybe Casey was sick after all.

"Hey." He caught up to her in a few strides. "What's wrong?" He reached out and took her hand.

Even upset, she was gorgeous. Those blue eyes pierced him, and raven hair framed her pixie-like face.

"I shouldn't have come," she said, but thankfully, she didn't pull her hand away.

He'd been thinking a lot about touching her lately. He'd never admit it, but she'd been the inspiration behind his newest collection. She was a combination of edgy innocence — at least she'd appeared that way when he first met her.

But that night in Greece that they'd slept together? Jesus. Innocence wasn't a word he'd use. Ever since then, he'd wanted nothing more than to call her, but she'd made it clear they were only using each other's body for that night and nothing else.

"What's wrong?" he said. "Is Casey all right?"

She stared at the ceiling. A single tear slipped down her cheek.

What the fuck? The tear tugged at his gut. Something was wrong. She wasn't the crying type.

"Everyone," he yelled to the small crew, who were milling around the set with his Ducati center stage. He always tried to get his bikes into the shoots. It was his thing. *The Times* had called his collections *Biker Chic*. "Take twenty. I need the studio."

He led her into his office, just left of where the shoot had been. "Sit down and tell me what's going on. Is Casey sick?"

"No," she said hoarsely.

"Okay." He opened the fridge behind the panel in the wall where he kept fabrics. "Do you want a beer?"

She huffed. "No. I don't want a fucking beer." Her hand flew to her mouth. "Great, now I have no impulse control. What the hell else is going to happen? I'm sorry. I shouldn't have come here." She rose, but then grabbed her head as if she were dizzy.

"Hey." He helped her back into the seat. "I know we aren't that close. But you can tell me anything. What's wrong?"

"I need to go home." She pulled her keys from her purse and started away, but she only managed a few steps before she had to lean against the wall to hold back the wave of emotion he could see coming over her.

"You're in no shape to go anywhere," he said. "Just tell me. Let me help you."

"You're not going to be any better at this than I am."

"You're not making any sense. Any better at what?"

She gestured to her body. "Can't you tell?"

"What is it? Are you sick?"

She gave him a look like he was an idiot. "I'm pregnant. With your baby. With your stupid, super-sperm-busting-through-condoms baby."

Holy fuck.

Chapter Three

In a way, Bennett felt a little sorry for Linc. She'd thought he was going to pass out in the chair there for a second. He sort of collapsed in on himself and ran his hand through his hair.

She remembered him doing something similar to her. How it had felt as he'd run his hand through her—

Oh my *gawd*. Not the time.

He stared at her as if assessing her in some way.

"The CVS bags were full of pregnancy tests?"

How the hell did he know that?

Probably Nick. Casey had refused to let him into the penthouse until they'd finished the tests. She couldn't believe he'd call Linc.

"Yes."

"How many?"

"What do you mean?" Did he mean weeks? He should be able to do the math on that one.

"Tests? How many did you do?"

Oh. "Uh, I think ten all together." Would he think less of her if he knew they hadn't done all ten tests at once? That they'd gone back for another three tests after the first seven had shown positive? "All pink, all plus signs. I was going to wait to talk to you about it until after I went to the doctor, but it was like a homing device drew me here. I'm scared. And Casey, bless her sweet little heart, was trying to help, but I think she's more scared than I am. She knows what a God awful mother I'm going to be."

"You won't." His shoulders straightened. "Be awful," he added. "You're going to be a great mom. You're smart and you're kind. Those are the two biggest things a mom needs to be."

She snorted. "So you're like an expert on mothers? What, was yours so perfect?"

His jaw tightened. Darn. She'd hit a nerve. She hadn't meant to. Grumpy had become her new state of mind.

"I mean—"

"I didn't know her very well. She died when I was young," he said, his voice low and thoughtful. "But my brother says she was those very things I described. She defended me to her death."

Wow. God, Bennett felt like a bitch. "Sorry." She wanted to ask more questions. Had someone attacked his family? But she'd been rude enough.

"You don't need to apologize. How would you know?" He stood then and sat on the desk in front of her. He took her hand in his and squeezed gently. "I'm going to be here for you, Bennett. I will be whatever you need me to be. I will take care of you and the babe, luv. You're never going to have to worry about anything."

She pulled her hand from his. "Whoa. Calm yourself, dude. I don't need any help."

That was pretty dumb. She was clueless about parenthood. Her mom had done her best but perhaps hadn't been the greatest role model.

"You will need help, though," he said. "And I'm the father. I will do whatever is necessary to protect you both."

What was with all the protection crap?

"I'll make some calls," he said. "We'll get you the best care possible."

"Uh. You're not such a good listener, are you? I got this. I have a doctor. Well, she's not an obstetrician. But Casey says she has a doctor friend who can help."

"Is it Jacinda?"

Bennett nodded. How did he know that? Had he dated her? He'd pretty much dated all of Dallas, New York, and Los Angeles. Not that she read the tabloids, but it was hard to miss his exploits on the entertainment shows. People loved the bad boy fashion designer who had a different girl on his arm every day.

Yep. And you're having his baby.

If she had a million dollars, she'd give it away to know what was going through his head. He had to be just as scared as she was.

"You okay?" He snapped his fingers in front of her face.

And just like that, she went from concerned to pissed off. "Get your hands out of my face, asshole. Yes, it's Jacinda. I'll go to the doc, but the rest of this crap you can stick up your ass."

She rose to leave and then grabbed the chair when a wave of dizziness hit her. Damn, pregnancy sucked.

His arms touched her shoulders, helping her to balance. She hated that his touch sent spirals of need to her—

No. Stop it.

"Fine. Do what you want, but I'm driving you home." He was all authoritative, and she was dizzy as shit, so she wasn't going to say no.

"Whatever."

The next day in Doctor Jacinda's office, Casey was on one side of the table, glaring at Linc, while he stood on the other waiting for the gynecologist and the sonogram. It was all Bennett could do not to giggle, which was weird since she was scared shitless.

Her best friend was furious with Linc for knocking her up. Bennett had never seen her friend so mad. She wouldn't have blamed Linc for staying behind just to save himself from Casey's wrath.

Yet here he was.

So fucking hot.

No man had ever made jeans and a T-shirt look so good. He filled the room with his presence.

"I'm sorry," Linc said softly.

She glanced up to see he was staring at Casey.

"You hooked up with my best friend. Out of all the women you could sleep with, you had to choose her?"

"To be fair, it wasn't all him," Bennett said. "I kind of seduced him."

"That's not the point," Casey said. "He's out with a different woman every single night. Now look what you've done." Casey pointed down to Bennett's stomach.

"You know better than anyone I don't sleep with most of the women I date. You *know* that crap is for publicity."

All of that was news to Bennett. She'd just assumed he was a man whore.

Casey patted his hand. "It's okay. I believe you."

He'd been really angry with Casey, but he glanced down at her hand on his and smiled. "And I told you, there's no way it could happen." He'd calmed down a bit. "We used condoms…" He shared a glance with Casey, like they both knew what he meant but didn't want to say it. "Besides, that night was…"

"A little crazy for all of us," Casey added. "I get that. But she's my best friend." Casey's hand went to her hip, but before she could say anything, the door opened, and the doctor entered. She didn't look much older than Bennett, and she had a kind face.

She held out her hand. "Hi, Bennett, I'm Dr. Henderson. You can call me Jacinda."

Bennett smiled nervously. "Hi. You know my friend, Casey."

The doctor shook hands with Casey, then gestured at Linc. "And this is…?"

"This is my, uh…Linc."

Eloquent as always.

What was she supposed to call him? Her friend? Her fuck buddy? The father?

"I've known Linc for years," Jacinda said and bumped shoulders with him.

What was that?

"And as for what to call him," she continued, "you guys

will figure it out. There's plenty of room in this modern era for whatever kind of family unit you two find works for you. I'm just here to help you confirm you're going to have a beautiful baby and when it will be. Are you ready for that?"

"If I say I'm not?" Bennett said.

"Then you can wait a few months and find out anyway, but I promise, this way's a lot easier."

Bennett laughed and squeezed Casey's hand. Her friend had said this doctor had a good sense of humor.

"I'm ready," she said.

Jacinda clapped her hands together. "Okay. Before we do the sonogram, I'm going to listen for the heartbeat. Lie back, please."

She took out a small, handheld machine that had a wand attached. She placed the cold tip of the wand on Bennett's lower belly.

There was a weird whooshing sound and then a fast *thump thump, thump thump, thump thump.*

"There it is, nice and strong," the doctor said.

A heartbeat.

No denying it now.

Shit just got real.

Linc grabbed her hand and squeezed gently. He glanced down at her with the strangest look in his eyes, almost as if he were in awe.

"All right, Casey, I need you to come to the other side of the table so we can do the sonogram."

Casey mouthed, "It's going to be okay."

Bennett didn't know about that.

The gel the doc had squirted on her belly was cold.

Linc rubbed his thumb across her knuckles, and the

action calmed her nerves.

The doctor turned on the machine and slid the silver ball across her belly. There was a clicking noise as she made measurements. The doc bit her lip and frowned.

"Is something wrong?" Bennett asked.

"Nothing at all. The baby is healthy."

But that didn't look like a nothing-at-all kind of face.

"Eight weeks since conception?" the doctor asked.

Bennett squeezed Linc's hand hard. To his credit, he didn't wince.

He was staring at the doctor with an intense focus. "If there's something wrong, you need to tell us right now."

Jacinda gave a gentle smile. "There's nothing wrong that I can see. Let me get these photos printed out for you and we'll have a more detailed conversation. I need to plug a few numbers into the computer, and then I'll have a due date for you." She handed some tissues to Bennett. "Casey, why don't you come with me to give them some time alone?"

Casey looked like she was about to argue, but then she caught another of those weird looks from Linc.

"Just give us a minute," he said.

Casey finally seemed to resign herself to leaving the room and exited with the doc.

"What was all that about?" Bennett asked.

Linc shrugged. "Here, you missed a spot." He took the tissues and wiped the goop off Bennett's belly. His touch sent all kinds of shivers through her.

"The doctor had a weird look on her face," she fretted.

Linc took both of her hands and helped her sit up. "There's something you need to know. About my, uh…medical history."

"What is it? Are you sick?"

He shook his head. "No. Far from it, actually."

"So what is it?"

He took a deep breath but didn't say anything.

"Jesus. Listen," she said. "You hesitating like this is making me more nervous than whatever it is you need to say. I didn't freak out—uh, much—when I found out I was pregnant. I can't imagine whatever you have to say can be any bigger. So bring it on."

He pursed his lips. "There's no easy way to say this." He turned away for a second and ran his hands through his hair. He'd done that when she'd told him about the baby, too.

He was always so confident and self-assured. What could trouble the most alpha man she'd ever met?

"You need to know now, before the doctor comes back in. Because when she tells you the due date, you're going to be shocked."

"Dude, did you take crazy pills this morning? I could tell you the due date on my own. We know when you knocked me up."

"Right, right." He shifted so he could sit on the edge of the table, but he didn't let go of her hands. "How open-minded are you?"

She had no idea where this was going, but a knot formed tight in her chest, which had nothing to do with the breakfast tacos she'd inhaled earlier.

"I consider myself pretty open-minded. I slept with you, didn't I?" she joked.

He grinned briefly, but then he was serious again.

"Have you ever wondered if werewolves, witches, and vampires were real?"

She had to stifle a laugh. The poor guy. The news of the baby had broken him. He was having a nervous breakdown.

"Linc, I didn't bewitch you or something. I mean, that night of the wedding I was hornier than I'd ever been in my life. But I didn't roofie you or anything so you could get me pregnant. The last thing I wanted was a baby."

He took a deep breath. "Yes, I remember you told me any guy with a dick would do. That's not what I'm talking about."

She tried to take the question seriously. "Do I believe in those things? No. I mean, I guess anything is possible, but you're talking about fictional characters."

"Sort of. I'm talking about the basis for fictional characters."

She looked at the door. Where was the doctor, anyway?

"The basis? I don't see where you're going with this," she said.

"You're expecting a nine month pregnancy. But the thing is, that's for human babies."

Hold on. Was he putting on some act so that she'd kick him out of her life? No. That absolutely wasn't going to happen.

"What the fuck is wrong with you?" Hell. She'd promised herself she'd stop saying "fuck" for the baby's sake, but desperate times called for graphic language. "I understand if you don't want anything to do with this. You don't have to pretend to be crazy. I can handle this on my own. To be honest, I'd *prefer* to handle it on my own." Jerk.

"I'm a werewolf. That's why you shouldn't have been able to get pregnant. I can't get humans pregnant."

Great. He was doubling down on crazy.

"Asshole." She shoved him hard, but he didn't budge.

Before he could explain further, the door opened and Casey and the doctor returned.

"Did you tell her?" Casey asked.

"I tried. She doesn't believe me."

"Can't say I blame her," Casey said as she sat next to Bennett on the other side of the table.

"You guys, this is not a funny joke. I'm already kind of nervous about all of this. You aren't helping." She again shoved Linc, who finally moved. She sat up and slid her legs off the side of the table.

The doctor motioned for Linc to sit down on the chair in the corner.

"There are things you need to understand," the doc said to Bennett. "I need you to take a deep breath and then listen carefully. Look at me, please."

Bennett stared into the doctor's dark brown eyes. She could have sworn they turned kind of an amber color.

Maybe I'm *the one going nuts.*

"Stay calm," the doctor said.

"Okay, you telling me to 'stay calm' isn't exactly helping. What the hell is the matter with all of you?"

"What Linc told you is true. He is a supernatural being, and because of that, your gestation period is a little shorter than normal."

Something had happened to her head. This was all a bad dream.

A weird wave of calm came over her. That was what this was. A bad dream. The wedding. The sex. The pregnancy.

The doctor snapped her fingers. "Look at me. Did you hear what I said?"

"Something about my digestion." Bennett's tongue felt heavy. "Am I having a stroke?"

The doctor put her hand on Bennett's shoulder. "You have about sixty days left in the pregnancy."

Bennett yawned. She should be panicking, but she felt so tired…

"What is wrong with you people?" she said. "I'm not so good with the math, but even I know that isn't right."

Casey grabbed her hand. "Bennett. The father of your child is a werewolf. Well, technically he's some weird Irish version, but potato, potahto."

Bennett cocked an eyebrow. "Yeah, and all of our friends are actually ghouls and goblins, too."

"Well…" Casey looked at Linc, who nodded at her, as though he was telling her to go on. "Actually, Nick is a sort of vampire-werewolf crossbreed, a Greek version. Doc here is a witch who can temper the emotions in a room. And I'm human, but I'm thinking about letting Linc bite me in a few years. It's a lot to take in. Believe me. No one knows this better than I do. But you're going to have a baby. And we can't keep this a secret from you because—Bennett?"

She pitched forward, but Linc caught her and cradled her in his arms. "It's all right, love. I'll keep you safe."

She glared at him. "You're a monster. I'm having a monster's baby."

And then she blacked out.

Chapter Four

Linc sat beside his bed and watched Bennett sleep.

She was so beautiful.

She was the mother of his child.

And she was fucking pissed off.

He didn't blame her. This was all kinds of wrong. He'd used a condom so she wouldn't have to worry, but the truth was that he shouldn't have been able to get a human pregnant. The magic that made him supernatural made it scientifically impossible. Which left one likely explanation. They'd know more after some of the blood work came back, but he guessed that Bennett might not be all human.

Funny how a life could change in less than a heartbeat. The crazy thing was, he liked Bennett. A lot. He was already intensely protective of her and the child. That was a part of his nature as protector, but that was all he could be.

He'd take care of her and the child. Make sure they never wanted for anything, but he could never be more to her than her child's father. But he'd die before he saw anything or anyone hurt Bennett or their child.

As for the baby, he would be the best father possible. His father had always been involved with pack or council business. He'd been a harsh man who thought Linc's choices were unseemly for the prince of the pack. It hadn't mattered that Linc had beaten down every wolf that had challenged his father's authority.

His father hadn't believed Linc had what it took to be a true leader. And maybe he'd been right when it came to the pack. But Linc had proven himself a successful leader in other areas of his life, especially with the council and Nick's army of supes. Now he'd be a good father to his baby. And God help whoever tried to stop him.

Bennett's eyes fluttered open. "Hey," she said.

He grinned. She'd gone a whole five seconds without calling him an asshole.

"How long have I been asleep?" She glanced around the room. It was decorated in his modern aesthetic, clean lines and no clutter. Definitely not the kind of comfortable place he figured she'd need.

He'd change that. Give her whatever she wanted. He'd make this place as comfortable as he could for her. He wanted her to feel at home.

"You've been out for a few hours, lass."

She put a delicate hand across her mouth and yawned. "Have you been here the whole time? Don't you have a fashion empire to run or something?"

"I had to make sure you were all right. What do you need?"

She shrugged. "All of this is…weird. I'm sorry I called you a monster. I mean, I saw the baby on the sonogram. It didn't have a tail or anything." She sighed. "We have a lot to talk about," she said cautiously, "but I still have to get my head around this. And I have about forty thousand questions for you about the…"

"Weird stuff?"

She bit her lip. "You won't hurt me or the baby, right? Like when the moon changes and stuff? That's all I need to know right now."

"No, it's not like that at all. Everything in the movies and television is wrong. I've had a few hundred years to learn to control my beast. I don't change with the moon. Hell, I can go years without changing." And he had when he'd been imprisoned a hundred years ago, after one of the battles he'd fought during the Supernatural wars. Though lately, he'd been changing twice a month to run on a ranch he'd bought north of Fort Worth. It was a great stress reliever.

She held up a hand. "Okay. I think the only way I'm going to make it right now is if you just let me ask questions a little at a time."

"Ask away."

"Nick is a vampire?"

Her calmness was impressive. "Right, but he's not a vampire in the sense you might think. He's Vrykolakas. He began as a wolf like me, but he went through a change hundreds of years ago, so now he's a bit of both. It increases his power, which he needs as the leader of the Supernatural Council."

She waved her hands. "Whoa. Okay, this is more complicated than I thought. But I guess as long as I know he won't hurt Casey, I'm good."

Linc chuckled. "There's zero chance of that happening.

He loves her beyond anything I've ever seen. He would give his life for hers."

"It's kind of sickening how into each other they are." She scrunched up her face.

"I'm with you on that. But it's in our natures. We're protectors. We look after the people we care about, no matter the cost."

"You did go kind of alpha on me when I told you. And, uh, you didn't even question if it was true. I still think that's weird, especially since you thought there was no way you could get me pregnant."

"You came straight to me," he said honestly. "You're an honorable woman, Bennett. I've seen the way you look out for Casey. If you thought there was a possibility of another father, you would have told me."

"Huh. Well, okay then. And no, no possibility. I'd been so busy with work since the wedding, I didn't even notice I was pregnant. So um...yep."

"So is there anything I can get you? Are you hungry at all?"

"If I can be completely honest...I kind of want a steak and baked potato."

Linc texted the kitchen downstairs to send up what she wanted and added his order to it. "Okay. I've sent the order for your food. What else do you need?"

"I'm okay. I can figure out the rest for myself."

He kneeled in front of her and put his hand on her leg. "Bennett. I know this is an awkward situation, but let me do this for you."

She bit her lip, like she was considering his offer.

"I'll eat here," she said. "But afterward, I need to go

back home."

He stood up. "About that. It'll be safer if you live here for a while." *Or the rest of your life.* But he didn't want to scare her. One step at a time.

If he just came out and said that, she might get the impression she was some kind of prisoner. Not at all. But he had enemies who wouldn't hesitate to hurt her as a means of getting to him. Like it or not, by carrying his baby, she was now caught in a world he was afraid she wasn't prepared for.

"I don't understand. I'm not going to do anything to hurt myself or the baby if that's what you're worried about."

"Right. I'm not worried about that at all, but you're carrying my child, and I want to make sure you're safe from any threats."

Her eyebrow rose. "*Now* what are you not telling me?" In the short time he'd known her, he should have realized nothing but the truth would work with her.

Where did he begin? How did he explain this without terrifying her?

"There are all kinds of supernaturals. I won't overwhelm you with just how many, but there are those who might want to hurt a child of mine."

"Why?" Her knuckles turned white as she fisted the blankets. "What did you do?"

"It isn't about what I did. It's about who I am. In my world, I'm royalty. There's always someone trying to take me out. It's not something I have to worry about every day, but that's because I'm careful. I have a security team that follows me around, much the same way they do Nick and Casey. You made fun of my posse before, but that's why they're always around."

Bennett stared at him. "Holy crap. So you're kind of a big deal?"

"I'm also Nick's second-in-command. There's always someone after him, too. That's one of the reasons most of us live and work in this building. The security is some of the best in the world."

She pulled her knees up and wrapped her arms around her legs. Linc's stomach sank—he'd frightened her.

"I don't know," she said. "It all sounds…suffocating."

He put a hand on her arm. She didn't flinch this time, which was progress. "I won't let anyone hurt you," he said, and he meant it. "I would give my life for you and our child."

She lifted her head and gave him a lopsided grin. She really was more beautiful than she had a right to be—and he was surrounded by beautiful women all the time. But hers was an organic earthiness that appealed to him.

"Let's hope it doesn't come to that." She took a deep breath. "I know I keep saying this, but it's a lot of change. I hear what you're saying, but I need my independence. Living here, well…this isn't exactly what I'm used to."

"What do you mean?"

"Um, well, my apartment is the size of this bed, for one. I mean, with the kitchen it might be a little bit bigger—but not much. I don't have anyone chasing me—except I once had a stalker ex. I tasered him and kicked him in the nuts. Last I heard, he'd moved to Canada with some chick."

Linc laughed. "I have no doubts you can handle yourself. And I want you to feel at home here. You can change things around however you want. This is my room, but there are three others. You can have whichever one you like best, and we can turn another one into a nursery. But I need to know you're here. Safe. And I understand your need for independence. But this isn't only about you any more. There's someone else at stake now. That means compromise. For your sake and the baby's."

She bit her lip. "I don't really have a choice, do I? Even if I say no and go home, you're going to send a team of security men, and my one-room efficiency is going to be very crowded."

Linc chuckled. "You have choices, but when it comes to keeping you safe, I'll do whatever it takes."

"What about after the baby's born?"

"After the baby's born..." He shrugged, trying like hell to seem nonchalant. "We'll figure out what works for you but doesn't put you in danger."

"And what about..." She raised her eyebrows. "What about us?"

A flash of sadness passed through him, and he looked away, hoping she hadn't seen it in his face. "There are some things...I can't offer. For your sake. For everyone's sake. It's a matter of keeping you safe."

"Uh-huh. So when we had our little adventure that night in Greece and said it was just sex, no romance, you were serious."

"Well..."

She smiled, like she was playing with him. "So if I wanted to go on a date with someone, you'd be okay with that?"

The suggestion hit him in the gut. Shite. He hadn't thought about that. And now that the image was in his head, he didn't want Bennett hanging off of anyone's arm except his own.

But it wasn't like he had any claim on her beyond this accidental pregnancy. Hell of it was, the way she made him feel was about as close to romance as he'd ever felt. But he knew why he couldn't go down that path. He'd just have to keep control over his urge for something more with her.

"If it comes up, we'll deal with it. Does that work?"

"Okay. And what about you? Are you going to be bringing women home? Because that could get a little awkward with your preggers friend hanging around."

He smirked. "So we're friends?"

She shrugged. "Seems like we should at least try for that."

"I have no plans to date anyone right now. I'm busy designing my next collection and promoting the one we have."

And to be honest, he didn't really "date" for the same reasons he'd never intended to be a father.

"So we're going to be friends who live together for now, at least until I have the baby. Then we'll figure things out? God, it sounds so simple, but this is some life changing shit."

"Lass, it is. But we're going to do it together."

She grinned. "Sometimes I forget you're Irish. Knocked up by an Irish werewolf, who happens to be one of fashion's most successful designers. I never do anything small."

He reached out and pulled her into his lap. There was something waifish and lovely about her that called to him. She settled in his arms.

"I'll take care of you and the babe," he whispered into her hair. "You'll want for nothing."

"I get that you need to keep the baby safe. But I don't want you to go all out for me. I just want to be as normal as possible."

He held her closely and breathed in her soft scent. He wasn't as sure about normal, but he would protect her. That was a promise he would keep.

Chapter Five

Two days later, Linc didn't know what surprised him more: how little a suitcase Bennett had brought into his place, or how quickly she'd rearranged everything he owned into a new configuration.

"More efficient this way," she said.

He stared at the empty place where his couch had once been. "Whatever makes you more comfortable."

"I know it's a little eclectic, but you'll see. You could use a bit of warmth in here. Everything is so sterile. For a fashion designer, your place is kind of plain."

Plain...? Everything had been arranged with purpose. The couch so that he could see every possible entrance into the place. The television so that it reflected a clear shot of the area behind him.

It's only for a few months.

Besides, the more comfortable she was, the easier his job would be keeping her safe.

"Clean lines help me to focus creatively." He tried to keep the judgment out of his voice.

She scrunched her face. "I'm the opposite. I need inspiration around me. Things that set my mind in motion."

He grimaced. He sure was staring at a lot of motion.

"Did you talk to Casey?" he asked.

She nodded. "Yep. For the time being, she and I are going to work from the penthouse. It's just easier."

"And the security guards?"

"It's going to scare the clients if they're standing around."

"But they need to be there."

She sighed. "Fine. But you tell them to be invisible. If we lose a client because they see some giant's shadow, I'm coming after you."

"As long as you'll let them do their job."

She glanced at him and laughed. "This is driving you nuts, isn't it? You're a good guy, giving me my space."

God, he loved her laugh.

Whoa, wait. Where the hell had *that* come from?

Get a hold of yourself, Linc.

"I told you I want you to feel at home. Whatever it takes."

She jumped up and tiptoed through the junk. She was wearing leggings and a giant sweater. No makeup, yet she was still beautiful. Without her normal platforms or heels on, she came to about midway up his chest.

"Bend down," she said.

He arched an eyebrow—what was she doing?—but did as she said.

She kissed his cheek. "This is some crazy shit we're dealing with. Dammit. I swore I'd stop cursing. Shit. This kid is going to be white trash happy if I can't stop."

Linc laughed. "I like it when you curse. Especially when it's because my mouth's on your—"

She hit him on his arm, and he laughed. He knew better than to bring up those kinds of thoughts about her, but the temptation had been too great to resist.

"I talked to Casey for a long time last night," Bennett said. "To be honest, I'm scared. Scared that I'll have a puppy instead of a baby. Scared someone's going to kill me before I can have the puppy-slash-baby. And scared that I'll be the worst mother in the history of mothers."

"Aw, Bennett." He hugged her. "You're going to have a baby, not a puppy. The wolf stuff doesn't happen until the teen years. I'm going to keep you safe. And you'll be an amazing mum. You're kind, funny, and generous."

"You're just saying that because you don't want me to have another breakdown."

"Everything you're feeling is normal. I'm expecting even worse."

She shook her head and backed away. "Gee, thanks."

He stepped around her and picked up *What to Expect When You're Expecting* from the coffee table. "To be honest, it's not just about keeping you safe. I'm thinking about everyone else, too."

"Is that right?"

"This book says that your hormones are going to make you homicidal at times. So by keeping you here, I'm protecting the world from you."

She laughed. "You may have a point. I couldn't get my suitcase open a little while ago and I was ready to rip it apart. Casey suggested maybe yoga."

Linc nodded. "I'll do it with you. I've got a great instructor. I'll have her come by tomorrow. And I had the guys set up an office for you in one of the bedrooms, and we'll set up the other one as a nursery."

"Wow. Nursery." She rubbed the bridge of her nose.

Linc winced—she *had* just said she was a bit overwhelmed. "Too fast?"

"A little."

"Sorry. We'll postpone any further nursery talk. You get settled. Make sure you rest. Anything you feel like eating, you can call downstairs and they'll bring it up. I'm borrowing Nick's jet today. I've got meetings with some buyers in New York, but I'll be back tonight. You have my cell. Casey will be here, but Nick's flying out with me. If you need anything, call me."

Bennett went to the corner where she'd moved his couch and sat down. "You guys are a little much. I've been on my own since I was seventeen and went to art school. I'm good. I don't need other people to cook or clean for me. Or teach me yoga."

"Got it." He smiled softly. "Tell you what, just for now, maybe don't be afraid to ask for some help now and then. Your body is going to go through a lot of changes really fast. Faster than a normal pregnancy. If you promise you won't overdo it, I'll try to back off. But you have to promise me something."

She eyed him warily. "What's that?"

"You'll stay within this building unless I can go out with you."

Her jaw dropped. "You're out of your mind."

"That's the deal."

"Or what?"

"There are people out there who would do you harm. You don't understand our world, but being Nick's second-in-command puts me in a spotlight of sorts. With our people, power is everything. And there are those out there who will do whatever it takes to gain power. I'm not asking this to make you a prisoner. It isn't a joke about people hurting you or the baby. Like it or not, I won't let that happen."

"I get that. I do. But I'm not going to stay in here until the baby's born. I'll go nuts. You can't expect that of me. And no one knows I'm preggers, so why are you so worried?"

He frowned. "There are spies everywhere."

"You're overreacting. The only people who know are you, me, the doc, and Casey—well, and probably Nick at this point."

"And everyone who has access to Jacinda's files in her office. Trust me on this, we have to be careful."

She crossed her arms in front of her chest. She wasn't going to bend.

"Okay. So. I'll just be gone today. Promise me that you'll stay here for that long at least. We'll figure something else out when I get back."

"I promise."

Something in her voice made him wonder if she was telling the truth. He'd have to put more men on her security detail. He would've taken her with him, but judging by the dark circles under her eyes, she really needed to rest.

Now more than ever, he needed to make sure he could take care of her and their child.

He lifted her chin in his hand. "You're scared. I am, too. But I'm here for you. Don't ever doubt that. I mean it."

She sighed. "I won't do anything to harm your child, if that's what you're worried about."

He gathered her off the couch and into his arms, and though he could feel the tension that she was trying to hide, she relaxed the longer he held her.

"That never crossed my mind," he said. "I'm talking about being here for you. I feel like I did this to you, and you're the one who has to go through the morning sickness and the pain of childbirth. I can't take any of that from you, but I can act as a resource. I can give you the things you'd otherwise have to struggle for. So please, let me make life as easy as I can for you." He kissed the top of her head. God, she felt good in his arms.

For a moment she stiffened again, but then she wrapped her arms around him. "Thank you," she whispered against his chest. Her shoulders dropped. "Hugs are good."

Fuck business. If what she needed was for him to be here, right now, he could reschedule a thing or two. "Do you need me to cancel my meetings today?"

She grunted. "As much as I'd like to stay like this for the rest of the day, you need to run an empire. And I have work to do as well. But thanks for offering. Now go."

He squeezed her tight, careful not to crush her.

A few minutes later, he exited the building. As he climbed into the limo, something tugged at his heart. His gaze travelled up the sleek, glassy exterior of the luxury apartment complex to the twenty-fourth floor, where she was.

Crap. He cared about her. Sure, he'd expected to have feelings for her. She was carrying his child. But he hadn't expected to feel like this. He had to maintain a certain level of emotional distance if he wanted to keep people safe. But this? How could he protect her if he cared so much? The thought of anyone touching her brought his blood to a boil. He'd murder the first—

Shite. He had it bad.

"I'm an idiot."

"What's new?" Nick asked as he climbed in the other side of the car.

"I don't even want to think about what I'll do when she really is in danger. And she fights me at every turn."

Nick tilted his head. "Getting attached, brother?"

Linc shrugged. "I don't know. I feel lost when I'm not with her. Could it be the child?"

"Perhaps. But she may be your mate. Odd, but it happens. If you're feeling an intense bond, she could be your fated match. We need to learn more about her father. I had the mother checked out, and she's as human as they come. May I dig deeper?"

"Would it matter? You're going to do it anyway."

Nick chuckled. "True. We can't risk unknowns right now."

"What did the blood test indicate?" Doctor and patient privilege be damned. Nick was head of the council, and he would know the results long before Bennett or Linc would.

"Inconclusive. It'll be another week or so before they know for sure, but she has magic within her. Which will help her with the pregnancy."

And what would happen when the council found out?

What would Bennett think if she discovered she was half supernatural?

She was already so overwhelmed. And if she was part supernatural, her magical ancestors might come for the child. In certain factions, the children were raised separately from the parents. And in others, they insisted the child *and* the mother live with them until the child was of age.

His fists clinched. He wouldn't let that happen. *Couldn't* let that happen.

Don't get ahead of yourself. Who knows? She might be half mermaid. Those fish people love to party.

Wouldn't that be a blessing in disguise? Even if it meant agreeing to weekly pool parties until the child was born. There were worse things than a race that didn't know how to do anything but have a good time.

"Whatever we find out, it stays between you and me for now. I don't want to cause her any more stress."

Nick pulled out his phone and dialed. "Mason, let's dig a little deeper."

Linc hoped they were doing the right thing. That old saying about the truth setting you free didn't always work in the world of supernaturals.

Chapter Six

Bennett hugged the pillow tighter. She'd have to put it back on Linc's bed before he returned. He'd think she was nuts if he knew the rich, woodsy smell of his cologne calmed her. They'd lived together for an entire month without killing one another. Each morning he hugged her and kissed her goodbye. That was one of the few times during the day when she wasn't in a panic. When she'd been wrapped in his arms earlier that morning, it was the safest she'd felt since all of this craziness began.

Don't get used to it.

As much as she craved security, it wasn't a part of her life. Her mother had constantly moved them around the country, never settling in one place too long.

But Linc going all alpha, promising to protect her… She kind of hated and loved it at the same time. No one was going to tell her what to do, but hell if she didn't like him trying.

Which was its own kind of trouble. But boy, just the

thought of his arms around her made her feel warm inside…

She glanced at the clock and gasped. She'd only meant to nap for an hour or so, but now it was nearly eight at night. She'd been out for almost four hours.

Stretching, she felt a bit light headed. The doctor and Linc had warned her about eating whenever she could. For the first time in two weeks she wasn't nauseous — she was starving.

She picked up the phone beside her bed and ordered a hamburger, fries, and a salad. Weird how much she craved meat, since she considered herself a most-of-the-time vegetarian. She hung up and glanced around the room. She'd made it as homey as she could, and she'd done the same with the rest of his apartment. He'd told her to make it her own… but what if he didn't like it?

After picking up the pillow, she headed to Linc's room. She'd just opened the door when he came out of the bathroom. Wearing only a towel.

His arms and chest were every bit as muscled as she remembered, and Jesus, those rock hard abs and the happy trail leading down between his legs…

Holy fucking hell, now that's *a man.*

Butterflies danced in her stomach. All this time, she'd managed to avoid seeing him any way close to nude. Because face it, she knew how her body would respond. Exactly like it was now.

"Lass?" He lifted an eyebrow.

"Um." She held out the pillow. "I was just bringing this back."

Please don't ask me why I had your pillow.

"If it helps you, you can keep it."

Shit. Why did he have to be so charming?

"Yeah. Thanks. It does."

The irrational part of her wanted to hate him for knocking her up—even though she played an equal role. But the rational part of her acknowledged that he'd done everything within his power to make her comfortable. He'd even let her sleep alone to "respect her independence."

She couldn't really admit to him that each night alone she fell asleep thinking of him, and sometimes it was all she could do not to go to his room and force him to repeat their one night together.

She chewed on her bottom lip, unable to look away. Why was she dressed in an old, extra-large Justin Timberlake T-shirt she'd found at a garage sale?

Why do you care? You are not, repeat not, *going to sleep with him again.*

But that didn't keep her from wanting him in the worst way. Her body craved his touch. The doctor had warned her that she'd have morning sickness, mood swings, and crazy cravings for the weirdest foods.

No one said being pregnant would make me into a horny teenager all over again.

"Bennett?"

"Huh?"

"Have you eaten? You look a little flush."

"I ordered—"

Something fluttered in her stomach, like a tiny tennis ball bounced around her organs. She reached for the bed and sat. "Holy hell."

Linc was by her side in an instant. She hadn't even seen him move.

"What is it?" he said. "Are you in pain?"

"Not pain. Just a weird—hell, there it is again." She put her hand on her stomach. "It's too soon, right? I shouldn't be feeling the baby. Something's wrong."

He put his large hand on her belly. The light caress of his fingers against her skin sent a shiver of pleasure down her spine.

Not the time. But damn, he was so close and smelled wonderful. Why were they sitting there instead of making out like crazy? She reached up to grab the back of his head.

Down girl, down—

Another flutter through her stomach had Linc off the bed and dialing a number. A moment later, he must have reached who he wanted, because he stepped to the corner of the room.

"She's feeling the baby," he said.

Bennett heard someone talking on the other end, but she couldn't make out the words.

"What?" she mouthed.

Linc smiled. "Okay. So no cause for worry. Yes. I'll tell her."

As soon as he hung up, she said, "Okay, what was that about?"

"Jacinda says it's not unusual. The baby's growing at an astronomical rate. In a normal birth, right now you'd be between the fourth and fifth month." He moved to his nightstand, opened the drawer, and pulled out a book.

Ah.

What to Expect…

He flipped the pages as he sat down. "I read the whole book last night. Even though you aren't showing much, the baby's probably pushing on your bladder. So you might need to pee more. And you'll start feeling those flutters more often. Spicy food or caffeine may make the child more active. Actually, you might want to lay off the caffeine altogether. They're still doing studies."

She crossed her arms. "Anything else I'm supposed to avoid?"

"Diet drinks."

She stared at him. An overprotective baby daddy was one thing, but denying her Diet Coke? That was crossing the line.

He made eye contact with her, and her heart skipped a beat. He was so close, with his addicting smell—and not to mention, he was practically naked. Hell, it wouldn't take much to get that towel off…

Shit. She needed to change the subject before she did something stupid.

"Well, that's super sexy," she joked. "My body is a baby making machine. So far as I can tell, I'm going to pee a lot and get super fat. Yay for me. At least I can eat everything I want."

He smiled softly. "You're beautiful. You don't need to worry about any of that. No matter what size you are, you're going to be gorgeous."

He couldn't mean it, but the words made her smile.

She patted his knee. "Save all the patronizing for when it looks like I have a couple of basketballs hanging out in my uterus. I might want to believe you about the beautiful stuff then."

She started to get up, but he pulled her back to the bed. And kissed her. His mouth closed over hers, and his tongue parted her lips. Dear God in heaven he tasted good. Peppermint and Linc. Limb-melting, crawl-on-top-of-him desire surged through her. She slid her hands down his chest, tracing the edge of hot skin just above the towel cinched around his waist.

Why was he always so warm? Was it a werewolf thing?

"You are beautiful," he said against her mouth. "So much so it's a distraction. I can't get you out of my head."

Then he deepened the kiss and pulled her on top of him. Hot. She was so hot all over, and she ached for him already. She moaned as his rock hard cock rubbed against her heat.

The idea that she had that kind of effect on him was a powerful aphrodisiac. She increased her pace, needing the friction his body provided. Craving it. And he was right there with her, rolling his hips in concert with hers.

He lifted his head and teased her nipple with his teeth through her T-shirt. Thank God she wasn't wearing a bra. Her nipples were so tight and sensitive that when his mouth closed over and he sucked, she trembled from her core to her fingertips and nearly came.

"Fuck." He rubbed his cock faster against her, straining against her wet panties. "This is what you do to me. Do you feel me? How hard I am for you? I've been this way since that night. You pop into my head, and the next thing I know I'm jacking off in the shower, remembering those tiny moans of pleasure coming from that kissable mouth of yours."

He'd been thinking of her? Like this? The same way she'd wanted him, night after night?

It was too much.

"Linc," she whispered, "I need you inside of me."

He chuckled as he trailed kisses up her neck. "Are you

sure?" His hands were on her ass, and he squeezed.

"Now. Do it now," she panted. How the hell could she be so into this guy? Her need for him had been bad that night in Greece, but not like this. She couldn't get enough of him.

He growled as he ripped her panties off and slid into her in one motion. So full. She was so fucking full, and he hit that spot, just there, and then he pounded up and down. His fingers teased her breasts. She arched back, her hands squeezing his thighs.

How many times had she wanted this? Craved feeling him inside her again. Dreamed about his hands on her. His fingers moved to the tiny nub at her core.

"Yes," she hissed. "Please."

Body quickening, she moved faster, and again he matched her. The pressure of his hand increased, and life became a haze of pleasure rippling through her over and over.

"Fuck," he said as she came around him. "So fucking hot." Then his muscles contracted and heat spilled out of him. He grabbed her shoulders and pulled her into his chest and kissed her deep and hard.

From far away, a bell rang.

"Dang. You're good. I'm hearing bells," she said against his lips.

He laughed. "It's the doorbell."

Oh! That's right. Food. She'd ordered the food.

And then everything was awkward. And if they didn't move soon, she'd have to grab him for round two.

"I should probably get that," she said.

"No. You aren't going anywhere. I don't want them seeing your just-fucked face. You're too beautiful as it is."

This time the compliment went straight to her heart. He

was acting jealous.

Probably just his natural protective instincts. He sort of made an art of being the alpha protector.

After sitting her on the bed, he grabbed the towel that had long ago fallen to the floor. While he was gone, she slipped into his bathroom and cleaned herself up. By the time she returned, he had everything set up in his bedroom at a small table by the window looking out on the Dallas skyline.

Funny, she wasn't as hungry as she'd been before. And, hello? Awkward? She was running around in no panties and she'd just had hot super sex with a man she'd sworn to never touch again.

He pulled out a chair for her. She yanked the T-shirt lower on her thighs and sat. He had put on a pair of jeans. Still no shirt. That torso of his was impossible. Who had abs like that?

Must work out every day.

"So." She grabbed one of the rolls from the basket. "That was hot, but weird. Right? I think I might have attacked you at some point."

The biggest clue was the red marks fading on his shoulder.

"That was mutual—I'm not sure what it was to be honest." Linc's eyebrows furrowed. "We should probably—"

"It's my fault." She cut in before he could crush her soul by saying they should never do it again. "My hormones are going crazy. I'm like some stupid teenager. I'm probably going to have to scratch that itch a lot, and I don't want to use you. I should probably date other guys or something. It's wrong for us to—I mean, you're the father and all but…"

"Bennett," he bit out her name. It was the first time she'd

ever heard him sound angry. She glanced up at him. "Shut up and eat your dinner."

"Hey, ass— Crap, I want to stop cussing. You can't talk to me that way. We need to talk about this like adults."

"Fine." He ground out the word. "The idea of another man touching you makes me want to break apart every piece of furniture in this room. And then I want to throw you up against the wall and fuck you so hard that you never even think about another man. How is that for adult?"

Shit. That was fucking hot.

• • •

Linc didn't want to upset her, but she'd struck a nerve. He'd just fucked her and she was talking about having sex with other men. He didn't want her to declare he was the love of her life, but she was having his baby. That should count for something.

"You sound like a Neanderthal," Bennett said. "You're okay if I use you like a human vibrator to get myself off."

"Being your sex toy doesn't sound like a hardship. Though if I'm not up to your usual standards…"

She snorted. "You're an idiot."

He stood and paced across the room. "I know what the problem is."

Please don't say I'm fat. Please don't say I'm fat.

"Ground rules."

Phew.

Wait…ground rules? She didn't like the sound of that.

"You don't want to feel like you're losing your independence. So we set boundaries right now."

"Okay… What were you thinking?"

He smiled. "We should be exclusive until the baby is born. Then we'll reevaluate."

She rolled her eyes. "Why are you looming over me? Being exclusive means we're in a relationship. And we're not. Right? Because neither of us does *long-term*. We might be in each other's lives because we share a child, but you can't tell me what to do."

Linc grit his teeth. "Bennett."

The woman was frustrating as hell.

"But for the next two months, I won't fuck anyone else while I have your child in my belly. Have you thought about how you're going to keep up your wolfish—pardon the pun—media persona? The paparazzi follow you like crazy. They're used to seeing you with a different model every day."

Relief rushed through him when she'd said she wouldn't fuck anyone else. It shouldn't bother him, but dammit, it did. And he wasn't in the mood to examine too closely why that was.

"We're having a child. I couldn't give a crap about my persona."

It was true. Bennett and the child were his only concern. He worried about them all day while he was away. Focusing at work had been nearly impossible. He'd fly people in before he'd leave her for more than a few hours again. The twinge she'd felt earlier when the baby kicked had nearly undone him.

That, and he might have missed his child's first kick if he'd stayed overnight in New York.

"Yes, but they don't know that."

He paused his pacing. "Speaking of, we can't say anything about the baby. The fewer people who know, the safer you are. Yet another reason you shouldn't be going out with other men."

She jabbed her fork toward him. "It's not like I'm going to run around and tell them I'm pregnant. I have a feeling that's probably a major turn off."

Not to him. Knowing his child was inside her made him feel all kinds of things, most of which he had no desire to examine.

"We share a child. That should be our focus for now. Sex may make things more complicated, but I'm willing to do whatever's necessary to help you through this difficult time." That's not what he meant to say at all. Why wouldn't his mouth work when he was around this woman?

She smirked. "Way to take one for the team."

He took her hands in his. "That isn't what I meant. I'll do anything to keep you safe, healthy, and happy. I pledge that to you and to our child. And a wolf's pledge is an oath of eternity."

She scrunched up her face in that cute way she did when she was thinking. "I have to warn you, I have a feeling my hormones may drive us both bonkers. That thing we just did? Almost made me cry. I never cry."

He leaned his forehead in so that it touched hers. "I can take it. As Casey likes to say, bring it on."

That made her laugh.

Linc sat in the chair next to hers. "There is something I need to talk to you about."

She hummed. "Is it a major thing? Because I'm not sure I can take much more. I'm kind of at my limit today."

He kissed her fingers. "Okay, then we'll wait until you're feeling a bit more settled."

She snorted. "Never mind. Now I'm going to wonder all night what you meant. Just give it to me."

He wasn't exactly sure how to tell her. "I don't want to keep secrets from you. I had thought it best that I wait until I had all the information, but...I suspect if you found out I was keeping this from you, you'd have my head."

"Jesus. It sounds ominous. Just tell me already."

"My kind can't impregnate humans."

She held up a hand. "Hold on. You're not pulling this shit now."

"Let me explain."

Her eyebrows drew together. "Go on..."

"You—uh, the thing is, lass, you said you never met your father. And you know for sure your mother was human. But in order for you to have my child, that would mean you'd have to be part...something else."

Her mouth dropped open. He put his fingers on her chin and closed it. She was eerily silent.

"Love, are you all right? Is it too much?" He knelt in front of her.

"I don't understand." She said the words so softly he wouldn't have heard them if he weren't a wolf.

"Your DNA tests will be back tomorrow. I thought it best to prepare you. You may be part human, but my guess is you're also part witch or fae."

"Fae? As in faery?"

"Aye."

She leaned over and put her elbows on her knees. "It's not going to stop, is it? This crazy train is never ever going to stop. You get that I don't want to know any of this, right? That this sucks? That I just can't— No. I don't care if I'm pregnant. I'm not going to cry again. This weird shit has got to stop."

He gathered her into his arms. He couldn't blame her. She had been through far more than any one person should in the last few days. She took some long, deep breaths, and he held her.

He'd give anything to save her from this pain, but she needed to know. Just like when he'd revealed his own supernatural essence, she'd be a lot worse off if she found out on her own.

"What's your favorite thing to do?"

She'd been quiet against his chest for a few minutes, but her arms were still wrapped around his neck.

"Eat. Paint. Draw. And listen to music. Not necessarily in that order."

Hmmm. "I happen to like those things as well. I have an idea. Throw on some jeans and a hoodie. I'll do the same."

She lifted her chin to meet his eyes. "I thought I had to stay in this prison because I wasn't safe."

"Love, it isn't a prison. It's a haven. And as long as I and a few of Nick's security team are around, you'll be fine. Now, get up and put some warmer clothes on. I have a surprise for you. You may not want to know this other world exists, but I think answers will help you. I know I could use a few. Will you trust me?"

"I look like crap. And I'm kind of tired."

"You're the most gorgeous woman I've ever met, and I promise this will be fun."

She gave an unladylike snort and punched his arm. "So

unnecessary. I know I look like hell."

Was she really so clueless? "Bennett, you're the most beautiful woman I've ever seen. Your eyes are the kind that make men go mad and begin wars. Your body's been burned into my brain since the day you changed in front of me for the wedding. Let me show you something."

He went to his desk and pulled out his sketchpad from the spring collection he'd been working on.

"Notice anything about my model?"

Hesitantly, she took the pad from him. Her eyes opened wider. "It's me," she whispered. "A much taller, slimmer version of me." She glanced up at him.

"Honestly, until all of this happened I didn't realize it was you. That night of the wedding, the night our son was conceived, your body, your smell, all of you was burned into my memory. For the last several weeks you've been my muse."

Pink tinged her pale cheeks. "That's just fucking crazy. Flattering, but crazy. You deal with supermodels every day. Women who get paid millions for cosmetics contracts."

"Maybe, but most of them need makeup and accouterment, as we like to say. But you're gorgeous in your yoga pants and vintage T-shirts. Now, go get dressed. I promise I won't wear you out, but you're going to love where I'm taking you. And there's someone who might be able to help us. No promises, but I feel like we should at least try to find out more about you."

She reached up on her toes and kissed him lightly on the lips. "Thank you. I think you're full of bullshit, but thank you."

With that, she slapped him on the arse and went off to

her room.

After getting dressed, Linc glanced around his apartment. Her crap was everywhere, but it didn't bug him. Not what he'd expected, given that he liked his life in perfect order and his surroundings sparse.

"Slight wardrobe malfunction." She lifted up her sweatshirt to show him that her pants weren't quite fitting around the waist. The small baby bump was keeping her from fastening them.

God, the idea that his child was in there excited and scared the shite out of him. He wasn't prepared for any of this. But then, neither was she.

"I kind of like you without pants," he said.

"Funny. I was trying to buy new jeans when I realized why my old ones weren't fitting, but in all of this craziness…I forgot to buy new ones."

"Not a problem. Give me a sec." He didn't wear underwear often, but when he did, he preferred boxer briefs. He picked a pair of dark blue ones out of his dresser and then went back to the living room. "Follow me to the studio. I have an idea."

She stared at the briefs in his hand. "Dude, you are fifty kinds of kinky, but okay."

Once in the studio, he ordered her to take off her pants. She did what he asked, and he went hard again. She was wearing a purple thong, and with those long legs…

Focus.

He cut a panel from the briefs and then sat down at the sewing machine. A few seconds later, he had created her a pair of maternity jeans. He held them up for her.

She laughed, a true and glorious sound. "I can't believe

you can do stuff like this," she said as she pulled them on. "Oh my God. They fit perfectly. I always think of you as such a manly man."

"You didn't when we first met at Casey's wedding. You thought I was gay."

She laughed. "I forgot about that. Well, you are gorgeous and stylish, and you know how to dress women. What was I supposed to think? But then you fucked me, and I never doubted your sexuality again."

That time it was Linc who laughed. "You never fail to surprise me. Now come on, or we'll be late."

Chapter Seven

Bennett strolled hand in hand with Linc through the Bishop's Arts section of Dallas. Local artists had set up booths to offer their wares and services. Bennett and Linc stopped at one of the three music stages to listen to a band she loved.

The fresh air and beautiful surroundings were a balm for her soul. A very troubled soul that was still trying to deal with the fact she was carrying a werewolf's child. And that maybe she wasn't who she thought she was.

Her mother had said her father was dead, but what if all of that was a lie? What if she had a whole other family out there? Why would her mother keep her away from them? She'd always wondered but never really questioned her.

"You're thinking too much again," Linc whispered into her ear. "There's someone I want you to meet." He pointed to one of the tents.

He'd been so sweet, even buying her cotton candy, which wasn't healthy for her or the baby, but dear God she needed it more than anything once she'd smelled it.

He led her into a booth filled with pottery, jewelry, and small terrariums. She reached out to touch a pitcher glazed in the most beautiful cobalt she'd ever seen.

"How do they get this finish?" she asked.

"It's a three-step process," a woman said from behind one of the larger pots. "One that makes the color richer each time." She had long blonde hair pulled up in a ponytail and a knitted green scarf surrounded her neck. Was she thirty? Sixty? Hard to say. She was beautiful in a natural, ageless way, and though her face was unlined, her eyes spoke of great wisdom.

The woman reached out her arms to Linc. "I've missed you."

"It has been a long time." He kissed her cheek. "When I saw your wares I knew it had to be you. I'm surprised you left your shop in Salem."

The woman shrugged. "The Council needs me here for the moment, so I thought I'd bring a few of my things and stay for a bit."

The council? "What kind of council is that?" Bennett asked.

The woman nodded toward Linc.

"I'll tell you more later," he said, "but basically all supernatural creatures must follow the laws of the Council. We abide by human laws to a certain extent, but we have our own as well." Linc smiled. "Bennett, I'd like you to meet an old friend of mine, Mikala."

Bennett and Mikala smiled at one another and shook hands, but Bennett had an odd feeling she was being assessed in some way that went more than skin-deep.

"Mikala, I want to introduce you to Bennett, who has

become very dear to me."

Dear to him? She glanced up at Linc. Damn, the man was a charming son of a bitch.

Mikala said, "I'd say she's very dear, since she's carrying your son."

Bennett gasped. "Son? How do you know?"

"Did Nick tell you?" Linc said at the same time.

Mikala laughed. "The day that vampire tells me something I don't already know is the day I hope the goddess decides my time is nigh."

"Witch, I didn't come here for you to peer into our souls," Linc said with a slight bite to his tone, but he was smiling. "I wanted to show her your art. Bennett is still getting used to the idea of our world. But you already know I also came for answers."

So this woman was a witch? Or was that just him saying something about her personality? Jesus, all this crap was confusing. She *had* said she somehow knew they were having a boy...

"Aye, I knew your real purpose." She squeezed Bennett's hand. "I won't apologize for my talents, but I didn't realize you had no idea. It's a great honor to carry a wolf's child, especially a son. There are so few of his kind left. I thought you'd be pleased it's a boy."

Linc sighed and shoved a hand through his hair. "I am." His voice was gruff with emotion.

Then he looked at Bennett with an expression she couldn't read. It was as if he were trying to tell her something, and though she didn't completely understand, she sensed the weight of his gaze, and it stole her breath.

"And I'm most grateful to her," he said. "But I came here

to help her understand her heritage, and to get a protection amulet."

Amulet? Like woo-woo magical crap?

"Something that'll cause no harm to her or the babe but will keep her safe. One that has a tracking spell attached would be helpful." He glanced away as if he were surveying the park. "I've never been so proud in all my life, and I want to protect them both in any way I can."

"You're proud?" Bennett whispered. "I thought all of this was more about duty than anything else. A responsibility."

"You thought you were a burden?"

She shrugged. "Well, yeah."

He hugged her. "I *am* proud, no matter what the sex. And I'm grateful to you for carrying my child."

"*Our* child."

"Our child," he repeated. "I'll admit I was surprised and perhaps a bit flustered by the news, but I'm excited. I haven't had family around in a very long time."

Wait, no family? "But you said you were from royalty?"

"Aye, I am. But I meant family in the way you might think. My mother died when I was born and my father went off to war when I was a lad." He paused and looked away. "He never came home. It was a few years later when Nick found me and took me in. He became my brother. An annoying pain in my arse, but a brother who would die for me. He kept me from self-destructing when I was cast out from my clan. When my father didn't come home, there was an all-out war for power—one I had no hope of winning."

"Not for lacking of trying." Mikala gave him a weak smile. "He had many opponents. He fought them. *All* of them. And he won. But it was a political game, and there was little he could do when the clan decided they wanted a new ruler."

"I—I didn't know," she stammered. Her voice came out more as a croak.

They'd both grown up feeling alone. Her mother had tried, but she was always at work, and they'd had no other family around. She understood that kind of isolation, and her heart went out to him. Hurt for him.

No wonder he felt so compelled to be the leader. The protector. The one who looked after everyone else.

He didn't trust people any more than she did.

That way, he never had to worry about opening up to anyone.

More than ever, she wanted to know about her father. She cleared her throat and turned to the witch. "Do you know what I am?"

• • •

Crap. Linc took a deep breath. It was one thing to come there looking for answers, but to actually find them was something else entirely. He placed his palm against the small of Bennett's back.

"I can tell you what you are," Mikala said. "If you truly want to know."

Bennett swallowed and nodded. "It's important to me. I just found out a few hours ago that I may not even be human. And I..." She put a hand to her head. "It's a lot. And now I'm not making any sense, and I'm kind of—can I sit down?"

Linc hated seeing her overwhelmed again. He scooped her into his arms and held her close.

"Let go of me, you big oaf. I don't feel *that* bad. Just a little dizzy. Probably the sugar from the cotton candy I shouldn't have eaten."

"Why didn't you tell me you weren't feeling well? I can take you home."

"Because I was fine until a few seconds ago. Now lay off." She looked again at Mikala. "Can you tell me?"

After a moment, Mikala motioned for them to follow her into the large tent behind the stall. "Dule, I need you to watch the front for me a bit." The black cat at Mikala's feet transformed into a young, twenty-something male with earrings and gauges in his ears. Dressed in leather, he looked like someone who might hang out in the hipster clubs in Deep Ellum.

Bennett shook herself. "Uh. That cat just turned into a man. I might feel sicker than I thought," she said as she sat on the large floor pillows.

Linc chuckled, relieved. If she was joking around, she'd be fine. "You didn't imagine it. Dule is a shifter."

Linc glanced up at Mikala, who gave him a knowing eyebrow lift. Crap. Whatever Bennett's heritage, it was going to be bad news for him. As one of his oldest friends, she'd always had his back, which made her concern all the more troubling. She wouldn't hesitate unless it was bad. Really bad.

Whatever it was, he could handle it. He was going to have a son. A *son*. He was a lone wolf with no clan. And even in the best of circumstances, his kind had a difficult time bearing young. He'd given up trying to find a mate long ago.

Bennett's shoulders trembled. He wasn't sure if she was cold or frightened. There was a neat stack of warm blankets near the pillows, and Linc grabbed one and draped it over her. Beside the sitting area was a small hotplate with a steaming kettle, and a table.

Mikala handed them each a cup of tea. Bennett peeked up from under her hair with questioning eyes, as if she wasn't sure whether she should drink it or not.

"It won't hurt the baby, but it'll help your nerves and nausea. I'll send some home with you. Carrying a wolf's child is strenuous work. You'll need to be able to keep your food down."

"Thank you," Bennett said.

"Calm your thoughts, wolf. I need to focus, and I can't do that if your emotions are all over the place."

"It's all right," Linc said.

Bennett frowned at him. "Are you nervous, too? Because as much as I want to know, I'm scared about what she's about to say."

"Drink the tea, both of you," Mikala ordered.

The hot drink warmed him from the inside out. He closed his eyes and sighed. Anxiety dropped off his shoulders. The witch's brew was a calming potion.

He opened his eyes again to watch Bennett. She took a deep breath. It was working on her as well. Good. She'd need to stay calm. He scooted closer and put an arm around her shoulders.

"Tell me first what you know of your mother and father's families."

Bennett shook her head. "Next to nothing. My mom and I were close, but she didn't have any relatives. She told me my father died before I was born."

"What was your mother's name?" Mikala asked.

"May," Bennett answered.

The witch frowned. "You said you *were* close. Is she gone from this plane?"

Bennett nodded.

"Give me your hand."

She glanced at Linc, and then held out her hand.

"Think about your mother. Picture her in a happy moment. One of your best memories of her."

Linc chewed his lip as she closed her eyes. Even with the tea, what if the stress of this was too much for her and the babe?

Mikala gasped and screeched. She released Bennett and bent over, clutching her stomach.

Linc reached toward Mikala. "Are you all right?"

"Don't touch me," she groaned. "She's bound by powerful magic. I wasn't expecting that—it's very well hidden. When I touched her hand earlier, it was easy to see into her and the child's minds. But anything about her mother is protected."

That wasn't good news. Powerful magic, magic even a witch couldn't see, meant only one thing.

Bennett was at least part fae.

His enemy.

And a woman he was sworn to protect.

Chapter Eight

"I think I feel sick," Bennett said as they walked through the lobby of the apartment building.

The news that she was part fae had sent her brain into the *Twilight Zone*. Her mother had been a faery, and not the Tinkerbell kind. All these years, her whole life, a lie.

She wasn't human. Linc guided her toward the restroom in the lobby. The security team at the front desk tried to act like they were invisible. Looking anywhere but at her.

"Not that kind of sick." She pulled away from him and headed for the elevators. She punched in the access code, and the doors opened to take them upstairs. "My head just hurts. I think I need to sleep for a bit."

He nodded.

"What does it mean? I saw your face when she said I was part fae. You went paler than a ghost."

"I was surprised, that's all." He leaned back against the rail of the elevator.

"Please, don't lie to me. From here on out, we need to be honest with one another. I can't take any more lies or half-truths. I need to be able to count on you to tell me the truth."

He glanced at the light counting off each floor, like he was checking to see how much time he had left in the elevator. "Bennett, you don't feel well, and there's no reason to cause you more stress right now. We can talk about it after you've rested."

"So it's really bad. I knew it. And there's no way in hell I'm going to be able to sleep now. Tell me."

The doors dinged open. He didn't say anything as they entered the apartment. She followed him into the kitchen, where he set about making hot, delicious tea. Whatever he was about to tell her, at least she'd have chamomile tea, right?

She sat on the couch—it really was better positioned in the corner—and waited for him to finish the tea. After a few minutes, he brought over two steaming cups and sat with her.

One sip, two sips, three sips…

"Linc, just tell me."

He put down his cup and started.

"Over a thousand years ago, there was a terrible war among the supernaturals. Everyone was fighting; witches, vampires, shapeshifters, and fae were all on different sides. It wasn't until we'd nearly hunted each other to extinction that the Council was formed. The governing body set up treaties between the factions. It came at a great cost, but for the most part there was peace."

"I've got a feeling peace didn't last," she said.

He shook his head. "About two hundred years ago, the

fae went after wolf shifters."

Oh hell. This was not going to be good. "Why?"

"The fae king's daughter had fallen in love with a wolf and they ran away together. He demanded the wolves return her, or he would kill them all. My people are proud and protective. They wouldn't give in to his demands, especially given that by then she was pregnant with the wolf's child. The fae promised they had only the mother and child's best interests at heart, but the wolves feared that giving her up would mean certain death for her and the child, because the fae have no love for wolves."

Bennett grimaced and picked at her fingernails. This story was definitely not making her feel any better. "So this was like a supernatural version of Romeo and Juliet?"

"Something like that. The Council stepped in to stop an all-out war, but not before there were heavy casualties on both sides. To restore the peace, the fae turned against their king and exiled him. They felt he'd put his own interest and his need for justice above what was best for their people. The new king signed a treaty with the wolves, but it included several clauses where the wolves and fae were to never cross paths again. That's an oversimplification, but to keep the peace, we're to stay separate."

Her stomach sank to her toes. "But…I'm fae and you're a wolf."

He grimaced. "Right. Though, technically, neither of us was aware at the time. And hopefully we can lean on that for mercy."

Mercy? He'd mentioned they might be in danger, but that was before all of this. What kind of mess beyond danger were they in now that they'd broken a centuries old treaty?

Fucking A, why was all of this so complicated? Sure, *she* would be the one to get knocked up and cause a war.

Thanks again, universe.

"So what does that mean for us?"

He shrugged. "I think Nick suspects you might be fae, but I have to talk to him. We'll need to go in front of the Council and plead our case. A lot has changed in the last two hundred years, but no wolf or fae has joined in all that time. Even though I was ousted from my old pack, they won't look kindly on my making this kind of mistake. They could make an issue of it, which won't be good for any of us."

"What do you mean 'mistake'?"

He shook his head and took her hand in his. "I only mean that this was an accident. I didn't know you were fae."

"Well, yeah," she said. "But there's no way you could have known, right?"

"They won't see it that way. As far as they're concerned, I *should* have known."

No wonder he'd been so nervous when he found out she was part fae.

She swallowed. "They won't kill us, will they?"

He set her teacup aside and gathered her in his arms. "No one will harm you or the babe, that I can assure you."

The funny thing was that, lying against his chest, she believed him.

"So what next?"

"Nick and I will make sure you're always safe," he said. "As your powers were bound and you thought you were human all these years, it's likely your mother was trying to protect you from something. But we have to go through the proper channels."

She sighed. She'd come into this desperate to keep him at a distance, but she had to admit—a baby on the way, a potentially disastrous conflict between the wolves, and the fae… It felt good knowing she wouldn't have to face it alone.

His strength seeped into her bones. And dear God in heaven, he smelled good. Even with everything she'd just learned, her body ached for him.

He chuckled.

"What?"

"Your hormones are kicking again."

"You can't possibly know that."

"Wolf senses. Can't help it. And as much as I would love to help scratch your itch, I really need to go talk to Nick. And you, lass, should rest. Come on, let's get you tucked in."

He picked up her tea and led her into her bedroom. After setting down her cup, he reached for the hem of her sweater. "Arms up."

She did as he said. He pulled the garment over her head and then hissed in a breath. His gaze was caught on her boobs, which were nearly spilling out of her bra. Just another benefit of pregnancy. "Fuck, you're beautiful."

A tight coil pulled between her legs.

"If you're going to leave, you can't say shit like that to me."

"Language." He kissed her jaw, then his lips moved up to her ear and he nibbled.

"Don't tell me what I can fucking say," she said as she reached for his belt. "And if you think you're going anywhere, you're sadly mistaken. I'm going to have my way with you. Then you can go."

She shoved his pants and boxer briefs down. His gorgeous cock sprang free.

He kicked off his shoes and pulled his sweater over his head so that he was gloriously naked. "Far be it from me to tell you no. But you have to understand, more than ever, that we can't let anyone else know about us. It puts us all in danger, especially you and the baby."

She shoved him back on the bed. "I'm not taking out an ad announcing anything. I just need you. Now."

And then she had her wicked, wicked way with him.

• • •

When they were done, he held her and let her rest her head against his chest. He took in a deep breath. All these years, he'd been a lone wolf, isolated for so long that he'd forgotten how lonely he felt.

But with Bennett in his bed and in his arms? He'd never felt so warm. So at peace. Like he was finally home.

"We should get something to eat," she said.

He kissed the top of her head. "In just a minute. There's something I want to show you."

She lazily looked up at him. "Is this going to end with us getting frisky again? Because you've really got to work on your lines. A playboy like you should have plenty."

Playboy. He couldn't fault her. Wasn't that what everyone thought? The media put him with a different woman every week, sometimes every day.

"I don't want to give you a line," he said. "I want you to see how much I love having you here and what I'm willing to do to make you feel safe."

"Okay…"

He'd planned on waiting a few more days before

showing this to her. But the moment was right. They were on an emotional high, and he wanted her to see what he'd done for her.

He led her to the third bedroom and opened the door...

She gasped. "What did you do?"

• • •

Linc flipped on the lights, revealing the most beautiful nursery she'd ever seen. Okay, she hadn't seen that many, but this one was definitely awesome. The walls were a soft buttery color and the furniture white. He'd left little eclectic touches through the room, such as animal vignettes painted on the walls and a toy box shaped like a treasure chest. But it was the blue chevron pattern on the bedding and the tiny airplane pillows that took her breath away. So much attention to detail.

"If you don't like it, or the colors, we can change it," he said quietly.

"Like it?" She stood on her toes and kissed him on the cheek. "Our baby is going to love this. It's like a wonderland." She went over to the treasure chest toy box and opened it. "Where did you find this stuff? And how did you get it here so quickly? We just found out he's a boy."

He leaned against the wall. Call him cocky, but he couldn't help but feel pleased at the smile on her face. "I've been making it since we found out you were pregnant. I started with the blue because it's my favorite color and it's calming. I wasn't really thinking about the baby's sex. But if you think it's too gender-specific, we can change any of it."

Eyes watering, she walked to the beautiful pearlized

crib and fingered the little blue and white stuffed airplane pillows hanging underneath tiny faux clouds. "Did you make those?"

"Yes."

There was a large padded rocker in soft blue in the corner, where she could rock the baby to sleep. It was the most beautiful room she'd ever seen. "It's perfect," she croaked out. "Wait… Did you make all of this by hand?"

"The truth is I couldn't find anything I liked, so I just decided to do it myself. It's more about my ego."

She laughed through the tears. "Don't kid yourself. You did it because you adore me."

He came forward and scooped her into his arms. "Well, you do make it easy."

She buried her face into his neck and laughed. "And I adore you. This takes so much worry off my shoulders. I couldn't imagine a better room for our baby."

He set her down but held her close against him. "I was worried that maybe I'd gone too far. I know you don't always like it when I take over. But I don't sleep much, and when I'm not working on the collection, I need creative distractions. This seemed like the right thing to work on."

She laughed. He was such an artist. Speaking of… The walls were amazing, but they were missing a little something. "Would you mind if I created a mural? Would that mess with your design too much?"

He put his hand under his chin and seemed to consider what she'd said, like he might actually say no, but then he smiled and she could see he was just giving her a hard time.

"Actually, I was thinking, when you feel up to it, maybe you could do it on the wall behind the crib," he said. "Give our son something to look at. I used non-toxic paints so it wouldn't bother you or the baby, and I have a ton left over you can use. I went through about twenty different colors before I settled on the wall color."

"You did all of this while I was sleeping?"

"Like I said, I don't need much sleep." He smiled at her and wiped her tears away with his thumb. "Do you still want to get something to eat?"

She grinned then pretended to snap her jaws at him. "Now that you mention it, I'd like another piece of you."

"You read my mind," he said.

He scooped her up into his arms as if she weighed nothing. There might be something to that wolfy strength. He carried her back to the bedroom and set her on the bed.

"You've got that hungry look in your eye..." she said.

"If you thought that last time we were in bed put you on cloud nine, wait until you see my secret werewolf sex trick."

She burst into laughter then pulled him to her. "Oh, this I've got to see."

Chapter Nine

As soon as Bennett fell asleep, Linc went upstairs to talk to Nick and Casey. As much as he wanted to stay in bed with her, they had to get this business of her heritage and the Supernatural Council sorted out before it spun out of control.

Nick was sitting on the plush leather sofa in his penthouse. "We'll need a solid strategy."

"I don't understand what the big deal is," Casey said. "This is the twenty-first century. You can have babies with whomever you want."

Nick squeezed her hands. "Humans can. And honestly, most supernaturals, too. But the fae and the shifters, who were part of the same world for thousands of years, have laws for a reason. They've never been able to get along."

"That's just dumb. We're all adults. Something that happened hundreds of years ago shouldn't dictate what happens today. It's archaic. You guys need to fix this. What if the fae want to come and take Bennett away?"

Linc's stomach twisted. That was his biggest fear. And who was Bennett's mother? She had to have been powerful, and for someone like that to run away from her homeland… That alone was huge.

"Did the witch have insight into who Bennett's family might be?"

Linc shook his head. "Bennett's full-blooded fae. The magic that made her appear human could only have been done by someone who—"

"Was incredibly powerful," Nick finished. "Possibly royalty. Hell. You know what that means?"

Linc bit his lip and stared out the window to the colorful Dallas skyline. It meant Bennett would be called home to her family to take her rightful place. Someone like her would be precious to her people.

"She isn't going anywhere," he said through gritted teeth. Selfish, perhaps, but he couldn't deny how protective he felt of her. Almost possessive. She wasn't the only one with an insatiable need, but his feelings went far beyond sex. Not that he was in the mood to examine those feelings too closely.

"Damn straight," Casey added. "She's my best friend. I'm going to be godmother of her child. She and that baby are staying close. Period."

"I agree," said Nick, "but it's going to take some political maneuvering the likes of which we haven't seen in some time."

In the reflection in the window, Linc watched as Casey planted a kiss on her husband's cheek. "Yes, babe, but you're, like, the dude. You can so make this happen."

Linc turned back to the couple. "I'll do whatever it takes to keep her here." He looked at Nick. "You're my brother, but you need to know that if this goes south, I'm taking her and we're running. I won't lose her or the child."

"Go you, Mr. Protective. I love it." Casey clapped. "So manly man."

"Understood," Nick said. "But let's try to do this the right way."

The right way seldom worked for Linc, but he would do as Nick asked. For now.

But his mind was already working every angle. Could he walk away from everything? Leave his business and his friends behind? He didn't know. Didn't *want* to know. But what he could say for sure was that if they forced his hand, he would move heaven and earth to keep Bennett and their child safe.

• • •

The Council had been meeting for more than two hours. Linc, with Nick's help, had stated his case. Stony-faced bastards hadn't said a word, only that they would deliberate on the matter.

Outside the chamber, he leaned against the wall. He'd refused to show any weakness in there. Strength was the only thing the Council respected.

"Linc."

He glanced up to find Meyer, one of the werewolves on the Council, coming toward him.

"You understand that no matter what the Council decides, we must all do what is necessary to keep the peace."

Including killing you and your child's mother.

Sure, that was a worst-case scenario, but Linc had gotten as far as he had by preparing for the worst. He hoped the Council would help him. But if they didn't? He would do what he had to do.

Still, that was no reason to pick a fight. Now was the time to play nice.

"Yes. I understand."

The wolf seemed to sense what Linc hadn't said—hell, he could probably smell the aggression coming off Linc— but he took him at his word, turned, and walked away.

Their future was up to the twelve people in that room, two of them fae.

He'd already prepared Bennett. Even though the circumstances were dire, he smiled when he thought about her reaction earlier.

"This is freakin' America. No one can tell me what to do," she'd said, her hands on her hips. She was fucking adorable when she was mad.

He'd already arranged for a plane to be ready, and his personal security team was prepared for his word. If the Council voted to send her home—which would be idiotic since they didn't even know which fae world she belonged to—they were ready.

He wasn't a man of faith, but he'd prayed. Held his heart to the universe and begged that the council choose wisely.

The door banged open and Nick burst through the doors, expressionless.

Hell.

Nick nodded for Linc to follow him out to the gardens. They couldn't talk inside. They were in the Council's mansion, and there were ears everywhere.

Once they were far away from the building, they stopped to talk. If the Council could eavesdrop on them all the way out there, they deserved to hear every word.

Nick crossed his arms. "You're safe for now since her magic has been bound and we don't know her heritage. But the fae are demanding we find out as soon as possible. They want to meet her."

Linc shook his head. He wasn't letting those assholes anywhere near her.

Nick sighed. "I've said she's on bed rest and doesn't need any more stress. They've agreed to wait, but I don't know how long I can hold them off. And honestly, we need to find out so we have some idea of who we're going to be dealing with."

"But if we unbind her magic, it could harm her or the baby."

"Which is why we're doing this the old fashioned way. Through her blood. I ran some tests when she was in before. The DNA markers show she's fae, but it'll take another week before the lab can discern what faction."

A week. Linc could plan a lot in a week.

"And the wolf thing…" Nick hung his head.

Crap.

"You won't be punished for breaking the treaty. You had no way of knowing. That said, it's a tricky situation. I was able to keep them from making any final decisions. But you need to be prepared, brother." Nick put a hand on his shoulder. "As much as I want to help you with whatever decisions you feel you must make, my hands are tied."

Linc understood. And in any case, he wouldn't allow

Nick to risk his Council leadership.

"You have to be Switzerland. I'm okay with that."

"Are you?" Nick frowned. "I'm not. Pisses the hell out of me. You're my family. You have been since the day we met."

Linc smiled. What a day that had been. They'd nearly killed each other before discovering they were fighting on the same side. "You have to think about the greater good. Sucks being the boss, but that's what you signed up for when you became the leader of the Council. And we need you there. So yes, I get it."

Nick sighed. "I'm glad you do. Casey's going to go berserker on me."

Linc smirked. "So don't tell her everything."

"Have you met my wife? Not a magical bone in her body, but she knows all. I'll walk in the house and she'll say, 'So why didn't you just crush those fae people and make them do what you want?'"

"Good luck."

Nick squeezed his shoulder. "It's going to work out. I'll do everything in my power to keep your babe and his mother with you."

And so would Linc. Even if it meant going against his best friend.

Chapter Ten

"What are you talking about? I've only been pregnant for like three weeks. It's not time for Lamaze yet." Bennett pointed a finger at the doctor. Linc kept mum. Even though her belly had grown in the last few days, delightfully so, she hadn't come to terms with the fact that this wasn't like a human pregnancy.

They'd had another sonogram. The babe was growing fast, and they were at the beginning of the third trimester. The morning sickness was gone, and for that he was grateful—he hated seeing Bennett suffer. She was a trooper, but the illness was making her weak.

The doctor helped Bennett sit up. "Yes, but you're in your third trimester. You have about three weeks until the baby will be here."

Bennett's eyes went wide. "Three weeks?" she whispered.

"Give or take a few days," the doctor said. "I told you the time would pass quickly."

Bennett bit her lip. "But Lamaze?"

"Yes. If nothing else, the breathing exercises will help you. And it's good to understand what's coming. I have a class beginning tonight. You would be the fifth couple in it, which is good. The smaller classes mean the instructor can give you more one-on-one help. Do you know who you want for your birthing coach?"

Linc held his breath. He wanted to be there. Wanted to see his child born and be the first to hold him in his arms. He'd watched a few videos online. What women went through… Fuck. He was glad he was a man. But in any case, he'd respect her wishes.

She turned to face him. "I'd thought about Casey for sure, but I'd like you to be there. I mean, the baby is yours, too. But it can get kind of gross, and a lot of guys don't like being in the room."

He smiled. "If you're okay with it, I'd like to be there. Two coaches have to be better than one."

"That's what I was thinking. I want to have all my bases covered. Is that okay? Can I bring them both to class?"

The doctor laughed. "Sure. It's actually not that uncommon. A lot of couples have one of them who travels for work, so they have a stand-in."

"Then it's settled," Bennett said. "Sign us up. And for the record, this is weird. Lamaze class. Wow."

"One more thing," the doctor said. "Before you leave… Nick mentioned you spoke with Mikala, but would you like me to confirm the sex of the baby?"

"Yes," Linc and Bennett said together.

They laughed and Bennett smiled at him. That grin of hers did crazy crap to his insides.

"So what are we having, doc?" Bennett asked.

Linc squeezed her hand.

The doctor brought up one of the pictures she'd taken on the sonogram machine. She clicked a few buttons and a picture printed.

"That…" She pointed to a tiny dot in the middle of the baby-like form. "…shows us it's a boy."

The smile on his face was so big it hurt. A boy. Blimey. It wasn't Mikala telling them. They had photographic proof. Which shouldn't have been more meaningful than the magical word of a witch, but somehow, the picture made it feel real.

"Cool. I mean…" Bennett paused. "I wasn't sure how I'd handle a girl. Always so much drama. But a boy. Um, cool."

"Very cool." Linc kissed her forehead.

"We're going to have a boy," she said. The awe in her voice was unmistakable. "I know your friend told us, but I'm not sure I believed her. But this is…"

He hugged her and sniffed. "Lass, I couldn't be happier."

She drew her head back. "You aren't crying, are you?"

He laughed. "Wolves don't cry. It's all this antiseptic, tough on my wolf nose."

"Uh-huh. If you say so."

"Nurse Cary will bring in the paperwork for the class. And I'm going to print up a new food list for you. I want to make sure you're getting enough protein to support the speedy growth of the child and the changes going on in your body. You can expect your size to increase rapidly from here on out. You may go up a size overnight."

"Why do I get the feeling I'm soon going to look like an Oompa Loompa?"

He hugged her again. "At least you won't be that weird color."

She snorted. "You always know what to say."

Linc turned to the doctor. "Jacinda, do you mind giving us a moment alone?"

"Of course. I'll be back in a few minutes." The doctor left.

Linc sat next to Bennett on the examining table. "It's a lot for you to take in. Are you okay?"

"Truth? I'm used to being on my own. I never rely on anyone but me. It works best that way. People usually end up disappointing me."

"Bennett–"

She held up a hand to stop him.

"Let me finish." She took a deep breath. "I'm not sure how I would have made it through the last few weeks without you and Casey. Seriously. About every ten minutes, I feel like I'm going to have a nervous breakdown. And then you're there. I'm scared to trust. I'm scared to depend on anyone. But right now, I need you and Cass."

"If it weren't for me, you wouldn't be in this situation," he said honestly. It wasn't the first time he'd voiced the guilt driving at him. It was a hollowness in the pit of his gut, knowing he'd put her in a situation that could get her killed.

He fucking hated it.

"True. Do you have regrets? I mean, I know you're on board; you've been really awesome about everything. But it must be a lot for you, too."

"No regrets." It was true. Even though they had a lot to work through, and there was still a ninety percent chance they'd have to go on the run, he had family now.

She put her hand on his heart. "Today, it feels real."

He smiled. "It does. How about you? Regrets?"

She shrugged. "Not really. I mean, I don't like what's happening to my body, or getting fatter. I'm already kind of uncomfortable. But there's a real baby in my belly. And it looks human, which, quite honestly, was a huge relief today. I know what you said, but I was scared it might have a tail or something."

He laughed. "I told you, we're all born looking like a human."

"I know. But come on, it's weird. To be honest, if I'm going to go through all of this, I'm glad it's with you. I never knew my dad. And my mom, she was great, but she was always working. When she died, I just felt so alone. And I worry that our baby might lose us. I mean, what if they decide we can't be together?"

"I told you, I won't let that happen." He put his arms around her. "I will protect you to my death."

"Shit. Crap. I mean, don't say that. I'd rather you save our baby. Promise, no matter what, that you will always put him first. Promise me, Linc, that you will always be there for our baby."

"I will. I vow it. But you can never ask me to choose. You are equally important to me."

Damn. It was true. She'd wormed her way into his heart. There was no way around it.

"I don't know what the future holds," she said, "but you're going to do whatever it takes to keep us safe. I haven't had that kind of security for most of my life. But right now, in this room, I feel safe with you."

He didn't think it possible, but his protective instincts

kicked into even higher gear. She was right. He would do whatever it took.

She pinched the bridge of her nose.

"Everything okay?"

"Yeah, just a little headache. I'm hungry, and I swear I still miss caffeine and chocolate. I don't think my body is finished with withdrawals."

"Let's check with the doc. Maybe you can have a little chocolate."

"Good idea."

Linc's phone dinged. Of all the times for someone to interrupt him...

It was a text from Nick.

DNA results are in. We need to chat NOW.

"What's wrong?" Bennett asked.

Then Linc saw the next text. It identified who Bennett's father was and, well...

He put his phone back in his pocket. "Lamaze class may have to wait."

He tried to hide his concern, but she knew him too well.

"Oh, fuck," she said.

You have no idea.

Chapter Eleven

"My dad is a king?" Bennett sat across from Nick and Casey in their dining room. Linc sat beside her, his arm around her shoulders. "That's, like, the most insane thing anyone has ever said to me."

"You're royalty. That part is kind of cool," Casey said, but she was frowning.

"Right. So what does this mean? Did he know I even existed? Maybe he didn't want me and that's why my mom left."

"He didn't know you existed," said Nick. "Your mother ran away before anyone knew she was pregnant. He thought she'd been kidnapped. They searched for her for years— even blamed the wolves, but nothing could be proven."

"And he lives in Ireland on an island that's protected by magic? What, are there leprechauns there, too?"

"It's not like that," Linc said. "The island is like Nick's in Greece, except it's warded to protect it from humans. They live much the same we do, but their magic is tied to the ley lines there, so few of them venture far from their homeland. The magic within them, within you, is tied to the earth, and there is no more powerful place for your family than where they live off the coast of Ireland."

"This is fucking weird."

Linc squeezed her shoulder. "There's more."

A few months ago, she'd have been happy just to know she had a dad. Now she knew she wasn't human. Oh, far more. She was fae. But it didn't stop there. Her father was royalty?

"I don't know if I can take any more," she said.

"Your father wants to meet you," Nick said. "I don't know if it helps, but he was as shocked as you were. I talked to him on the phone. He never denied it might be true. When I told him your mother's name, he didn't recognize it at first. And then he asked what color your eyes were. When I told him they were almost navy blue, there was a long pause. And then he said he had to see you."

She'd given up on the idea of a father when she was five. As Bennett had grown older, she'd figured, whoever her father was, her mother was afraid of him. She'd assumed he was a bad guy she didn't want to meet.

But now?

What were you thinking, Mom?

Her mother wouldn't have put them through the hell they'd lived in on the road if she hadn't been afraid of something. She may have lied to Bennett about everything, but her mother had also been protective.

"With all this craziness, could he hurt us more? I mean, hell… I don't even know what I mean. I don't trust him. My mom kept me away for a reason."

"I won't let him harm you," Linc said with a low growl.

"We don't even know what he wants," Bennett said. "But it makes me nervous. What do you think?" She glanced up at Linc.

"I can't make this decision for you. But I, too, am nervous about bringing anyone else in at this point. It could be a power play. Or it might be a father finding a long lost daughter. Whatever you want, that's what we will do. I'll keep you safe no matter what happens."

Why did everything have to be so fucking hard? As much as she wanted—*needed*—her independence, she had to admit that the way things were looking, she needed Linc, too. She'd come to rely on him in ways she'd never expected she'd rely on anyone.

But this was also her first chance to connect with the father she'd never known, and Linc's presence—loving and protective though it was—wouldn't help put her Fae father and the wolves at ease with an already tense situation.

"I don't know why my mom left my dad. She never told me. I mean, she told me he was dead. But after all this time, I need to talk to him. I need you to give me enough room to do that. Linc, you have to back off the alpha crap. You've been great. And you say you'll respect my wishes, but your eyes are saying something else. I have this feeling you want to throw me over your shoulder and run to your private plane to whisk me away to God knows where."

Casey and Nick glanced at each other.

Linc growled. "You aren't wrong. But I will respect your wishes." He ground out that last bit.

So protective, that one.

"And you have to respect that I'm not the kind of girl who lets anyone get away with anything." She poked him in his rock hard chest.

"True," he said reluctantly.

"None of us will let him hurt you," Casey said. "He can't do any woo-woo crap, right? Or kidnap her? Cuz if that happens, I'm going to kick all kinds of ass. Assuming Bennett leaves anything for me to kick."

God, she loved her best friend.

Nick sighed. "Calm down. They'll meet in an area where his magic won't work."

She shivered. Was her father really so powerful that they were worried he'd whisk her away?

Just another boulder on the mountain of crazy. Every time she reached the limit of how much she could take, there was more.

"I'll meet him," Bennett said. "But with Linc and you guys with me. I want every bit of security we can have in place. But you keep your distance, got it?"

Nick smirked. "Yes, ma'am."

Linc coughed. She glanced up to find him hiding a smile. "What?"

"There aren't many people who can get away with talking to the head of the Supernatural Council like that, save his wife."

"Oh, sorry. Was that kind of bossy? I forget you're not just my best friend's husband. I guess I'm a part of your freaky world now."

"I'm used to it." Nick nodded toward his wife.

"Damn straight." Casey crossed her arms. "Nothing will happen to you. He'll have to come through Linc, Nick, and then me. Maybe not even in that order. He messes with you, I will personally kick his ass."

"If he can get through me first." She pointed to her belly. "Nobody is going to mess with us. Even if Linc's made me so fat I can't see my feet anymore."

She and Casey high-fived across the table.

"All right. I'll put it together. He'll be here tomorrow." Nick said.

Her new bravado faded. "So soon?"

"I'm pretty sure he boarded a jet the moment he hung up with me. He could have used magic to get here faster, but I think he wanted to give you time to absorb the information."

That had to mean he might not be a total bad guy, right?

So she was going to meet her father—tomorrow.

Holy hell.

· · ·

"The place is reinforced with iron rebar. There's no way he can use his magic," Nick said for the third time.

Linc paced back and forth in his studio. Bennett had fallen asleep hours ago. Linc had tried to work—his new collection wasn't going to design itself—but he couldn't focus. He'd asked Nick to come down to go over the plans again.

"And the witches are on board? They'll do the wards?" Linc asked again. The security set up for the next day would be as tight as possible. He'd called in almost every favor owed to him to make sure of it.

"Yes. Brother, she'll be safe. And we'll all be there. He tries anything, Council leader or not, I'll rip his bloody throat out."

"You'd have to get in line. Why does this shite have to be so fucking complicated? Why did she have to be fae *and* his daughter?"

Given this latest turn, Linc was certain the universe hated him.

"They killed my pack. My whole pack, Nick." He'd left that part out when he told Bennett about his past. He'd been cast out, but twenty years later, the fae had attacked.

"It wasn't him. It was that asshole Dickens, the Mad Fae. He wasn't acting under anyone's orders when he took out your village. The truce had been called. You can't blame Bennett's father. Dickens was a madman acting on his own."

"So everyone says."

"Linc, you need to remember this about Bennett's father. You didn't hear him on the phone. He was in shock, but he was happy. The king has no heirs. I guess, after Bennett's mom, he didn't want to try again to have a family. We might be enemies with the fae, but when it comes to his people, they adore him. He's a just ruler."

"And ruthless. One of the most ruthless warriors in the war."

"Weren't we all? We can't fault any man for doing what's necessary during battle. We've killed just as ruthlessly."

Linc growled. Dammit. He didn't want logic. He just wanted to keep Bennett safe.

"I've got to get back upstairs before Casey wakes up and finds me gone. I promise you, brother. We've got this." He patted Linc's shoulder and then left.

Nick had better be right. They'd known peace for two hundred years, but Linc would wage an all-out war to protect Bennett and their child.

Bennett was his, and no one, not even her father, would come between them. Treaty be damned.

Chapter Twelve

"I'm going to throw up," Bennett whispered to Casey, who stood next to her in the most formal ballroom she'd ever been in. Not that she'd been in that many. The room was elegant, from the enormous gold and crystal chandeliers to the polished teak floors. A reception area had been arranged at the head of the room. Later, there'd be a party to welcome her father officially to Dallas, but for now, it was Linc, Casey, Nick, and her.

Oh, and about twenty of Nick's security team stationed around the room. That was a deal breaker for Linc.

Casey squeezed her hand. "You're pregs. You can't say that unless you mean it."

"True. Linc will come running with a bucket."

Casey chuckled. "He does like to take care of you. Never thought Mr. Playboy would fall to his knees for any woman, but you have him wrapped around your pinkie. You should have seen him barking orders earlier."

"He's just worried about the baby."

Casey smiled. "You keep telling yourself that. He watches you like a hawk, trying to anticipate your every move. And then he has the most adoring look when you're talking. It's the cutest thing I've ever seen."

Bennett rolled her eyes. "You've had romance on the brain ever since you and Nick hooked up. I know he loves his son, but I'm just the vessel. He's fond of me, and I feel the same way about him. We make a good team. But there's no romance."

Casey gave an unladylike snort. "You're so clueless. You think he's so protective of you because there's no romance?"

Bennett started to say something but was interrupted by the opening of the double doors.

Linc moved behind her and rubbed her lower back, soothing her.

A handsome, dark-haired man entered. He was tall and wore a fancy blue suit. She'd guess Armani. Looked to be in his mid-thirties. Probably one of her father's flunkies.

He paused in the middle of the room as if he were taking it all in, and then his eyes found her. He cocked his head and stared at her with penetrating blue eyes.

What the fuck?

He strode to her, pausing a few feet away. "Bennett?"

This couldn't be her father. He was too young. Too handsome.

She nodded. Her stomach crawled up her throat, making it impossible to speak.

"I'm Alex Thorngood, your father."

And then Bennett did the only thing she could. She puked all over his very shiny shoes.

Half an hour later, Bennett and her father were seated at the far end of the ballroom. She'd had to force Linc to move across the room. He'd refused to leave her side, but she wanted time alone with this man who claimed to be her father.

He'd changed clothes, as had she. And the cleaning crew had already made her little mishap disappear. Thank God the floors had been wooden.

"That wasn't exactly how I wanted to say hello," she said. Mortified, she tried to smile.

"Ah, lass, they didn't tell me you were with child. We could have made this all a bit less stressful for you. I apologize." His Irish brogue was even heavier than Linc's.

"I don't think there was a way to make it less stressful for any of us. I think this was just nerves. I didn't know you existed."

He glanced at the table. "That makes two of us. I had no idea I had a daughter." Then his eyes met hers again. "But I'm beyond happy to find out I do."

"It's weird. I'm not going to lie. I've lived my entire life believing—" Her throat caught. Tears burned the back of her eyes.

Not now. You've already lost it once.

"Why? Why did my mother leave?"

His eyebrows drew together. "I have no idea. She disappeared the week before we were to wed. We were bringing together two very powerful clans to form an alliance. She'd never liked the idea of being involved in politics. But we'd known each other since we were children."

"Wow," Bennett said. "You were in love even that young?"

Her father smiled, but there was a hint of sadness in the expression. "The match had been made by our parents, but we'd grown to love one another. We'd demanded that we be allowed to plan our wedding and follow through on our own timeline. And then a week before the wedding, she just disappeared. We thought she'd been kidnapped. It very nearly launched another war."

Her mother had to have been mistreated in some way. She was a kind woman and responsible by nature. She wouldn't leave her family behind without a good reason. At least, Bennett didn't think so. Her stomach tightened with worry.

"But she was pregnant with me then. She had to have been. So why would she just leave?" The question had plagued her since she'd found out she had a father. "Was it anything you did?"

"No!" Everyone who was discreetly eavesdropping at a table forty feet away looked at them. He waved a hand. "Sorry. For years, I went through every moment with her. She was nervous about the wedding. She didn't like the idea of being a queen. The responsibility weighed on her, but I thought she had come to terms with it. The truth is, I can't tell you why she left. And since she didn't tell you, and she bound your magic, I can only guess she hoped you'd never discover your heritage."

A headache formed behind her right eye.

Mom. You couldn't leave a note?

But the one thing her mother had given her was a fierce independence. Her mother had been trying to protect her in the only way she knew how. Sucked, but that was the truth of it.

"So what happens now?"

Her father clasped his hands on the table. "I'd like to have a chance to know you. I realize traveling in your state might be ill-advised, and I can only be away for a few days. But now that I'm here—now that we're reunited—I'd like for you to come home. To take your rightful place by my side. No matter what the council decides, I can keep you and the babe safe."

She thought she heard a groan from the other table. She glanced over as Nick put a hand on Linc's arm. He wouldn't be happy about her taking their child anywhere, especially if he couldn't come with her. And it wouldn't be fair to him.

"About that. Uh. Like mom, I'm not really the royalty type. We lived paycheck to paycheck. And I'm about as common and regular as a person can get. I mean, I'd like to get to know you to understand my heritage. But I just found out about this whole other world, and I won't take the baby away from his father."

Her father glanced over at Linc, a sudden tension in his expression and his voice. "The wolf is the father?"

"How did you guess?"

"He hasn't let you out of his sight since I entered the room."

Right. And Linc was a wolf. And her father was fae.

"I know your kind and the wolves have had some... difficulties in the past."

Her father didn't immediately respond. Which said it all, didn't it? He was choosing his words carefully, as cautious about saying the wrong thing to her as he was about saying the wrong thing where others could hear.

"It's not a question about what happened between us in the past. It's a question of where you'll be safest. It's a question of what's right for you and the baby. The wolves… Their world… You don't know them the way I do."

"You're right, I don't know them well. But I do know Linc. He's as honorable as they come. While I wasn't exactly looking to become a mom, my kid couldn't have a better dad. So you need to back off any talk about taking us away. I just met you. Father or not, I don't know you."

Her father's lips formed a thin line.

Whatever. She wasn't backing down.

"I do ask, before you make any major decisions, that you give me the opportunity to show you my world. To introduce you to what it means to be fae."

She wasn't making any commitments. A buzzing had begun in her brain, and her limbs were fatigued. A wet noodle had more energy than she did.

Who knew meeting your pops would wipe you out?

"We just met, and you're my father, so I'm going to be honest. I won't make any promises I can't keep. As curious as I am, I have more than myself to think about now." She placed her hand on her growing belly. "But I promise to consider what you've said."

"I can't ask for more than that." He stood up as though to leave, but then he turned back to her. "This wolf. Do you love him?"

"I care about him."

Her father seemed to consider that. "You know the history of our people and the wolves?"

"Yes. Not so great."

"So you know that our clan is responsible for the death of his pack?"

Bennett's stomach churned as her heart slammed hard against her chest. "What?"

He took her hands in his. "I'm sorry. I thought he told you and that's why you were reluctant to come home with me."

Her breath caught. "Why would you kill his people?"

"It was done without official orders, by a madman who very nearly caused the end to the peace talks. The fates have an odd sense of humor. You're carrying the wolf's baby. His new pack. I suppose there's a bit of life's circle at work there."

Her people had killed Linc's family. It had been hundreds of years ago, but she couldn't help but feel responsible in some way.

A very tall and thin man who reminded Bennett of a stick bug walked up. "Sir, the Council would like to meet with you before the reception."

Her father frowned at her. "Unfortunately, I must go. I would much prefer to use this time to get to know you, but it's been many years since I've traveled to America. And I cannot, no matter how much I want to, forsake my duties."

As much as she didn't want their chat to end quite yet, she needed a break. A nap. Her headache wasn't getting any better.

"Will it hurt your feelings if I don't stay for the reception? I'm not feeling so great."

He put a hand on her shoulder. "Has all of this been too much?"

She took a deep breath. "Yes. But it's good. I'm glad we have this chance to get to know one another. I promise I don't want to leave. Just the idea of standing around with so many people wondering who I am and why I'm here—that's kind of my idea of hell."

His smile disappeared. "Your mother was the same way. She didn't like crowds or…" For a moment, he seemed lost in the memory of her mom. "You should rest. Will you allow me to see you later? Perhaps in the morning? Will you have breakfast with me?"

"I'd like that." And she meant it. She wasn't sure what she'd expected, but he wasn't it. "Can I ask you something?"

"Anything." He kept his hand on her shoulder as if he were reluctant to let go.

"Why aren't you old? You've been around a couple hundred years. Is it magic?"

He chuckled. "One of the beauties of your heritage, lass. We age very slowly. I'm eleven hundred years old. And with the wards and iron, which are like handcuffs to our kind, I couldn't glamor myself a spell even if I wanted to. You rest. We'll talk tomorrow."

As he strode through the door, the power emanated from him. Every eye in the room followed him.

Casey ran up and nudged her shoulder. "Your dad's kind of hawt."

"Shut up."

"It seemed to go okay. I mean, you're still here. And you both smiled a couple of times."

Bennett smirked, as she nudged her friend toward the door. "You were sitting at a table with a wolf and a vampire who have supersonic hearing, don't pretend you don't know every word that was said."

"Not *every* word. But we got the gist." Casey looped her

arm in Bennett's as they headed into the hallway. The place was a gothic masterpiece down to its ornate sconces on the wall.

"Why would my mom leave him? When he was talking about her, I could see the hurt in his eyes. He wasn't angry, he was sad. He still misses her." Her mother had chosen a life of hardship as a single mom. She had no education, so she worked as a waitress and housekeeper. Always with two jobs, sometimes three. On one hand, Bennett understood why she'd make so many sacrifices to keep her independence. But leaving the guy who had to have been the love of her life? It didn't make sense.

What had been so bad that she'd had no other choice but to leave?

"Maybe he said something and doesn't remember. She was pregnant, and you know better than anyone that hormones can make you think funny stuff."

"Yes, but she never tried to contact him. Never went home again. Not only did she abandon him, but she never saw her family again. And I remember her talking about her brothers and sisters and how much she loved them."

It had been a long time ago that she'd had a conversation with her mother about family. She'd been twelve and had to write a paper about her family tree. "They're gone, and we can't see them anymore," her mother had said. Gone. Not dead.

All these years she'd thought she was alone after her mother died. But she had a family. A father. What was so awful that her mother would deny her the one thing she'd wanted most?

Chapter Thirteen

"I'm calling the doc. You're too pale," Linc said as he opened their apartment door. "This has all been very stressful. You've been through too much the last few weeks." He sounded like a mother hen, but he couldn't help it. As he'd watched her talking to her father, he'd been scared.

Some small part of him had hoped her father would be an asshole she hated. That wasn't the case. While it had been tense at first, they'd warmed to one another. She liked him.

Dammit.

"It's not your fault," she said.

"What?" He hung her jacket in the coat closet.

"Me getting knocked up. And today, me feeling over-whelmed. None of that is your fault."

She was probably right, but he couldn't stop blaming himself. He should have realized she was special. He'd been drawn to her from the first time he met her.

Might have something to do with the fact she was

fucking fae royalty. Even with her powers bound, she would draw others to her.

"If anyone should feel at fault, it's me. Why didn't you tell me what happened to your family?"

"He had no right to tell you about that."

"He's my dad. He can pretty much tell me whatever he wants. It was some crazy dude, but still. They took everything from you." She wrapped her arms around his neck. "If it makes things weird between us, I'll understand. I'm sorry. I don't know my family, but I feel responsible somehow."

He pulled her tighter to him, breathing in her sweet, cinnamony scent. Her warmth sank into his chest, calming his nerves. "You always smell like apple pie to me."

She giggled against his shirt. "Smooth way to change the conversation."

Speaking of… "Let's get some food into you."

She sighed. "Can we finish this first?"

He tugged her gently along behind him and deposited her onto one of the barstools. "If we must. But I'll say this once, and I don't want to discuss it again. I came to terms with what happened to my family years ago. And Nick reminded me it wasn't the actions of your family or clan. It was one man and his army of assholes. So I don't blame him. What I'm angry about is him wanting to take you away."

"I'm not so sure I could be as grown-up about it," she said. "I'd be pretty pissed that one of my dad's men killed your family. As for the other stuff, you heard what I said. I'm not going anywhere you can't go."

Linc arched an eyebrow.

"Pissed isn't cussing. You say that about people who are drunk."

He shook his head. "I was thinking more about how he said he could protect you. He's right. No one could reach you there. But I'll fight for you, Bennett. On my honor, I will."

It didn't matter whether he trusted the fae. Which, of course, he didn't. The safest place for Bennett and her baby was here, with him. Wherever she went, he would go. If they wanted to take her from him, they would discover the power of an overprotective werewolf father.

She snorted and then patted his chest. "Down boy." She giggled. "Stop being so alpha, dude. I meant what I said. Not going anywhere you aren't welcome. And sure as hell not leaving my friends. Casey needs me."

He willed the hair along the back of his neck to soften. "Sorry," he said. "You can't blame me for being so concerned."

"My new pops is just as alpha as you. He's just trying to be all, 'You'll do what I say, young lady.' And he has no rights. Doesn't matter what my mom did. He has no power over me. No man does."

She gave him the patent-pending Bennett squinty eye.

He turned away and headed into the kitchen to make her an omelet. God, he loved it when she had her ire up.

She came in and leaned against the counter while he cooked.

"What a day. I actually puked on his shoes."

"As first impressions go, I doubt he'll forget it."

She rolled her eyes at him. "Thanks."

He cracked a couple of eggs into a bowl. "I do what I can."

"He wasn't…"

"What you expected?"

"Definitely not. Did you know he'd look like that? He could have been one of the dudes on your runways. I think he might look younger than I do."

Linc finished whisking the eggs and poured them into the omelet pan with the mushrooms and tomatoes he'd been sautéing. "I can tell you he doesn't." He flipped the omelet.

"He's a king, but he didn't act super royal or anything. He seemed like a regular guy. Well, kind of. There's something about him."

After sliding the food onto a plate, he handed it to her. "Power like his is hard to contain. The wards and iron tamped it down. But I have no doubt that had he wanted to try something, nothing could have stopped him. Scared the hell out of me."

"You don't scare easily."

"No. I hadn't been frightened in ages until you came along."

She laughed. "Me? Why would you be afraid of me?"

"Not of you. *For* you. When you were so sick. And then you've been through so much. I worry about you all the time. I've cared about people, but never anyone as much as you."

The words came out before he realized what he was saying.

Crap.

He hadn't planned on that kind of declaration. Not to her. Not even to himself. But now that he had made it, maybe knowing the depth of his feelings would convince her to let him do his job as her protector.

She stopped chewing. "Linc, that's so sweet. But the baby is okay. He's growing strong. You saw the sonogram."

She didn't get it.

"I wasn't talking about the baby, Bennett. I was talking about you." He made his way around the breakfast bar. "You need to know..." He put his hand on her belly. "Yes, you're the mother of my son, but you're also my friend. More, you're my lover."

She cocked her head to the side. "I care about you, too. But stop worrying. I do get overwhelmed at times. But I have my friends and you. I'm not sure what I'd do without you guys."

Linc's stomach sank. *Friends*. Was that all he was to her? Why was he disappointed?

For now, it would have to do. He wouldn't push the issue. The last thing she needed was him pressuring her about something he wasn't sure about himself.

"Hey, earth to Linc." She snapped her fingers in front of his face.

"What?"

"I'm feeling better. I don't need a nap."

"Good," he said. He had to get her to stop thinking about her father. "We missed the first Lamaze class. We should go."

"Lamaze? Uh. Okay."

She pursed her lips, and he caught himself staring. God, how he wanted to kiss her.

"I made breakfast plans with my father. And I'm nervous about the baby thing. The kid's going to be here in a few weeks, and I'm really not at all ready. And we should probably get some stuff for him. Like blankets. Babies need blankets and diapers. Oh God. What kind of diapers? I mean, I'm all about the environment, but not if I have to do five hundred loads of laundry a day. And they don't eat right away, do they? I mean, they suck on your boob. Well, not *your* boob—"

He put his hands on her shoulders. "Take a breath. We're doing this together. And I've read a lot. I have no more experience than you, but we can handle this."

She leaned into him and exhaled. "Thank you."

She deserved someone so much better than him. He could care for her, but he had a feeling the only way he'd get beyond *friend* with her was to offer the love and marriage thing.

He was confident he'd be a great father to his child, but he'd never been very good at relationships. He'd have to satisfy himself knowing he would be the protector she and their son would need, the kind he'd dreamed of his own father being.

If only he could be something more. But he'd broken enough hearts to know that it was better to keep his distance now than hurt her later by pulling away.

If only his heart were thinking the same thing.

Chapter Fourteen

"And breathe out, in staccato, *huff huff huff,*" the midwife/instructor ordered. She was more of a drill sergeant than the kindly nurse he'd expected.

"Are you sure we can't leave?" Bennett muttered between staccato breaths. "Having a baby can't be this hard. Women do it all the time. I mean it's not cake. But Jesus, how are we going to remember all of this? We should just go."

Linc gestured toward the midwife. "You want to deal with her?"

"Isn't that what you're for?" She leaned up. "My big strong protector."

His gut tightened. "Let's at least learn what we should be doing," he encouraged. "Just in case we need to breathe on the way to the hospital."

He was talking out of his arse, but he did feel this was important. Birth was painful. When they'd first arrived, they'd watched a video depicting childbirth, and he'd cringed right along with Bennett.

"Now find your focal point."

"What focal point?" she asked harshly.

Linc bit back a smile. "We're supposed have brought a stuffed animal or something. I forgot in the rush to get here. He fished around in his pocket and pulled out a hundred dollar bill. "Here, focus on this."

She twisted her neck to give him the Bennett eyebrow.

"Next time I'll bring the stuffed animal. It's temporary."

She sighed and leaned into him again, practicing her breathing. "This is harder than it looks. I feel kind of woozy."

"Then stop." He waved to the midwife. "She's dizzy."

The woman knelt down and put her face in front of Bennett's. "Take a long, slow breath in through the nose, and then out through the mouth. That's it. Again."

Bennett did as she asked, even if she didn't look happy about following orders.

"Better?"

Bennett frowned and grumbled but nodded.

"Good." The instructor pointed a finger at Linc. "Now you, as her partner, need to count to make sure she's only doing the heavy panting during the contraction. As soon as she stops, instruct her to breathe normally."

"Yes, ma'am."

Bennett giggled, and then coughed to cover it.

"Wench," he whispered.

She laughed again. "It's nice to see someone giving *you* orders for a change."

Now he laughed, too.

The drill sergeant—er, midwife—gave them an irritated glance.

"Some of you may not be comfortable in the sitting

position," the midwife said. "So let's get on all fours. Partners, sit in front of the mother. Pull her attention to you."

Linc moved around to sit in front of Bennett.

She didn't look so happy. "Is there any dignity in giving birth? At all? Could this be any more mortifying?"

He had a feeling these were rhetorical questions and anything he might answer would be misconstrued.

"You're doing great," he settled on saying.

That's what the book had told him to do. Stay positive. The mom-to-be might turn into a screeching banshee and try to rip your balls off, but it was important to stay positive and keep a level tone.

"Take in a long breath, and hold. And then begin the pant," the instructor barked.

By the time it was all over, Bennett was exhausted. When they walked outside, the security team waited to escort them to the SUV. Linc wasn't taking any chances with her father in town. They'd have armed guards until the man left again. She might have liked her father at their first meeting, but he didn't trust the man.

"Are you hungry?"

She glared. "When am I not?"

He pulled the list out of his pocket and read through the dietary items listed. Dairy, proteins, fruits, and vegetables. He was about to start typing on his phone, but then she cleared her throat.

"I want Greek food. Hummus and tzatziki. And dolmas, the little grape leave thingies. And baklava. Oh, and some of those Greek olives."

Linc kept his head down, hiding his smile as he typed the list into his phone. At least she had a healthy appetite again—it meant she was getting stronger.

"And a milkshake. Chocolate. And don't tell me I can't have chocolate. It's one fucking milkshake. Crap, I cussed. I know, it's too much sugar. But I want a bite of the baklava, and the baby really wants a milkshake."

Mason, Nick's head of security, was driving. His shoulders were shaking. Linc prayed Bennett didn't notice, or Mason might lose his head.

Linc cleared his throat. "Got it. And as far as I'm concerned, you can have whatever you want."

She gave him a quizzical look. "Since when?"

"Always. You're a grown woman. You can decide what's best for you."

She rolled her eyes. "You're trying to act all not-so-alpha so I won't think about going with my dad."

Stabbed straight to the heart.

"So you are thinking about it." He kept his voice level, but he wasn't feeling it. No, anger burned deep.

She didn't answer him. "How long until we're back to the apartment?"

Mason cleared his throat. "About thirty minutes."

She pushed the button to raise the window between them and the driver, and then turned to Linc. "Do you trust me?"

"Yes." Where was she going with this?

She took his hand in hers. "Then listen to me. I promise you that I won't take your child away. I've lived without my dad my whole life. I have no idea why my mom kept me from him, but I won't do that to my kid. You and me? We make decisions about the kid together. Okay? So we decide what keeps him safe. We decide what he eats. We decide where he goes to school and if he can watch cartoons and read comic books. Which, for the record, he will."

"Yes, ma'am." He saluted her. Her words helped assuage his fears a bit. But there was a part of him that wondered if maybe being away from him might keep her safer. He knew better than anyone the kind of dangers he could face as Nick's second-in-command.

But he knew, too, how Bennett had railed against him even suggesting she hide out in his penthouse until after she'd given birth. He couldn't imagine how angry she'd be if she went to the realm of the fae and learned how shut off it was from the rest of the world. No one in, no one out. Not without the king's say-so.

For better or worse, she was going to stay with him.

"Okay," she said, then curled up and put her head in his lap.

Only a few seconds passed before he heard her soft and slow breaths. She was already asleep. He chuckled. The midwife must have worn her out more than he realized.

He gently moved the wisps of hair from her cheek. She was letting it grow out, and the prenatal vitamins helped. It was already past her chin.

He thought about the way she made fun of her own appearance, and the self-conscious way she assessed herself in the mirror each morning. She was fucking beautiful, and she didn't know it.

Never in his life had he cared more for someone.

She sighed and snuggled into him.

She was his woman. When the hell had that happened?

First time you met her, arsehole.

She'd been invading his dreams, even serving as his muse, but he hadn't seen it.

Did she deserve a better man? Fuck yes.

But she was his. And no one was taking her away.

Chapter Fifteen

"Does everything look okay?" Bennett rearranged the flowers again on the dining room table. "I shouldn't have moved
all my crap in here. It looked so much better when it was just
your stuff. He's a guy, and he probably likes clean lines, like
you do."

Nerves of steel, that one. Linc was having a hard enough
time keeping the growl out of his voice. He couldn't help it.
This was his place. No, *their* place. Their territory. And her
father was coming into it.

But being on edge wouldn't help the situation. She
wanted to form a relationship with her father? Linc wouldn't
stand in the way.

But that didn't mean he had to trust the guy.

"Everything looks beautiful," he said. "And I love your
stuff—it's made my house a home. Now it has the Bennett
touch."

She blew out a breath, walked over, and wrapped her

arms around him. "You're sweet. I'm going crazy, and I don't know why. He seemed like a perfectly nice man yesterday."

"He isn't going to care about the flowers or the artwork. Though, I want to make sure he knows the one over the fireplace is yours. It's my favorite."

She slapped his chest. "Stop that. You're going to make me cry. I need you to be your regular mean, sarcastic self."

"Ah, lass, please don't stress. I think if you don't puke on his shoes, we'll call it a win."

"See, that's what I need right there. You're right. I wish you could drink when you're pregnant. I mean, if ever there's a time you need to calm your nerves or deal with hormones…"

"It's not even nine in the morning." He groaned internally as soon as the words slid from his mouth.

Wrong thing to say, Linc.

"Don't be so effing judgy." She paused and actually reached around to pat herself on the back. "See, I knew I could get a handle on this cussing problem." She looked back at Linc. "Of course I'm not going to drink—I want to have a baby with a brain. Otherwise he won't be able to fight all the women off. Jesus, if he looks anything like you, we're going to have to beat the girls off with sticks. I think there are laws for that sort of thing."

"Bennett." He pulled out one of the barstools. "Sit."

"Don't tell me what to do ass—jerk." But she sat.

"We have a good fourteen years before we have to worry about dating."

"Eighteen," she said through gritted teeth. "Maybe not until he's twenty-one. That's a good age for dating."

Linc bowed his head so she couldn't see his smile.

"Twenty-one. So let's practice the deep breaths, in and out."

Her eyebrow shot up. "You're managing me. I don't like to be managed."

"That I am, lass. But it's not me being bossy. It's me keeping your blood pressure down. Now breathe."

She took a deep breath and closed her eyes. "Promise me he won't date until he's twenty-one."

"I swear to uphold whatever you think best." He wasn't making any promises he might have to break later. Poor kid. Bennett had worried about being a good mom, but she was already a protective hen. The boy would be lucky.

"Okay. I'm really worried about this co-parenting thing. I mean, after he's born, I'll be in my own place. And—"

The doorbell buzzed.

"Fuck, he's here. Shit. I cussed. Dammit."

"Breathe," he ordered again. "I'm going to get the door. You're going to sit here and pull yourself together. He's your father. He wants to see you. Last night, you got on famously. Now calm down, or I swear to hell I'll send him away and tell him you aren't feeling up to it."

Nothing would give him more pleasure. The less time they spent together, the better in his eyes. Aye, he was a selfish bastard, keeping a girl from her pa. But she was his girl.

"You wouldn't." Her big eyes rounded.

"Oh, I would do anything to protect you. Don't doubt that."

"Go, go." She shooed him away. "I promise, I'll be good."

Linc snorted, but he left her to answer the door.

• • •

Bennett squeezed her hands together, willing herself to calm down.

Don't puke on him. Don't puke on him.

Damn, she needed a different mantra.

Once she'd pulled herself together, she met the men in the living room. They both stood when she walked in. Her father wore jeans and a sports jacket over a white button-down. If she hadn't known who he was, she might have mistaken him for one of Nick or Linc's friends dressed for a casual Saturday.

He reached out and took her hands in his. She hesitated—should she kiss his cheek? Give him a hug? Maybe not. They weren't *that* friendly yet.

So she played it safe and just smiled. Her father smiled back.

"We have breakfast coming up in a few minutes." Her voice was much calmer than she felt. At least it'd been a full thirty seconds without her throwing up on him.

"Thank you," he said. "I didn't want to put you to any trouble."

"You aren't. Please, sit." She motioned to the couch.

"Would you like me to go? You two have a lot to talk about," Linc said.

She had to give it to the guy. She could tell from the tone of his voice that the last thing he wanted to do was leave them alone, but at least he'd offered.

"Actually, I'd like you to stay." She needed his strength. And he made her feel brave. "If that's all right with you?" she asked her father.

"Of course," he said, smiling softly. "May I ask how you two met?"

"Casey is my best friend, and she's married to Nick, who is Linc's best friend. They're so close that they call each other brother."

Her father arched an eyebrow. "The head of the Council is your best friend? That's a powerful ally to have."

What an odd thing to say. Did he think Linc was friends because he wanted to use Nick in some way? Was that how her father thought? Friends were just allies?

Linc straightened his shoulders. "He was my friend and fellow warrior long before he had any power."

Her father nodded toward him. "I did not mean to offend, wolf."

Bennett coughed. Way to get on the guy's bad side. Hell, way to get on *her* bad side.

"His name is Linc."

"Apologies again. Now I've offended both of you."

Linc smiled. It looked forced, but it was there. "I don't mind the term. I'm proud of my heritage."

"Point taken. I only meant that we're in an odd and potentially difficult situation with you and my daughter. It's good that you have friends with a political edge. And I talked to the fae on the council, who also seem to appreciate your talents."

Talents? What talents?

Linc raised an eyebrow and pursed his lips. Maybe the talents thing wasn't a compliment. "I've helped to keep them safe for more than a hundred and fifty years," he said, his voice rising. "Through all of the wars. I'm willing to do whatever it takes to protect those under my care—"

"*So*, you live in Ireland," she interjected. Something was going on, an undercurrent between the two men, but she was clueless to understand it.

"Yes. You'll love it there. It's lush, and I've never seen a more beautiful place in all the world. Wouldn't you agree?" he asked Linc.

"Aye, it's beautiful. Though I've never been to *your* island." Linc's brogue grew heavier the more time he spent with her dad.

Breakfast arrived—thank God—and they moved to the dining room. Eggs. Fresh fruit. Coffee for the boys. Oh, how she longed for the day she could drink coffee again.

They sat at the end of the long table, but as delicious as the food smelled, she was too nervous to eat.

"May I be blunt?" her father asked.

Bennett stopped pushing her eggs around her plate. "Of course."

"It's uncomfortable for me that my unmarried daughter is pregnant and living with the baby's father." He turned to Linc. "There's been no commitment ceremony, and I want to know your intentions toward my daughter."

Heart racing and fists clenched, it was all she could do not to spit at him.

How fucking dare you.

"Jesus!" Okay, not as tactful as she'd intended, but this had to be said. "You just found out about me two days ago. You don't get to come in here and make judgments. He's done nothing but take care of me. He invited me into his home, let me throw my crap everywhere, held my hair back while I puked my guts out for days on end, and put up with every crazy whim I've had. He didn't ask for this, but he stepped up to the plate. Unlike you, asshole."

Both men stared at her like she had two heads. Okay,

great. At least now they had something in common.

"I'm sorry about the asshole part," she said. "I'm trying not to cuss in front of the baby. But if you think you have any say in my life, you're wrong. I invited you here today to get to know you. But you have no right to tell me how to live, or with whom." Her hands shook. "And now I'm pissed off, so I'm going to my room. That's right. I have a separate room. But if I want to fuck—dammit." She shook her head. "If I want to sleep with him, I will. You need to go."

She turned on her heel with as much bravado as she could muster and stormed out. And then, like the true grown-up she was, she slammed the door.

She sat on the edge of the bed and put her head in her hands.

Fuck. That had *not* gone as planned. But he'd gone too far, acting like he had some ownership in her. Maybe her mother had left because she couldn't stand his pushy, overbearing ways.

He was insufferable, insulting Linc like that, and making her feel like a whore.

A few seconds later, there was a light knock on the door. She didn't bother to answer because it opened and Linc popped his head in the room.

"Is he gone?"

Linc had the nerve to smile. "No, I asked him to finish his breakfast."

"I don't want to talk to him. He doesn't get to come in here and judge us."

He sat next to her and put his arm around her shoulders. "It wasn't a judgment. He was just stating that he was a bit uncomfortable."

She looked at him with not a little suspicion. "That's rich coming from the guy who was half ready to go full wolf on him."

Linc shrugged. "I'm trying to do the right thing here. We're *all* uncomfortable with the situation. He's a little more formal in the way he speaks than you're used to, but no less blunt. I think you were ready to find fault because you didn't like how he was talking to me."

"He called you 'wolf.'"

Linc grinned. "That he did. And it's true. Look, he's had no contact with my kind for hundreds of years. There are laws that prevent that sort of thing. And now his daughter is shacked up with one. You have to understand that he's worried. He's just found you, and now because of these laws that are in our treaties, he's worried that he might lose you again."

"Why?"

Linc shrugged. "It's tough to change minds. When he was talking about Nick, he didn't mean it as a way to use him, he meant it as a way to protect us. We broke a law without knowing it. When you come into your magic, if you choose to have it unbound, there will be some very big decisions to make."

He walked over to the bassinet that would soon hold their son. He shook his head, reached in, and picked up one of the stuffed animals. A wolf. Cute.

"Honestly, I don't want to defend him," he said. "I'd prefer he leave and never come back. I'm a greedy bastard. I want you for myself."

She got up, came close to him, and put her hand on top of his. "I'm not going anywhere."

"You say that. But I can feel you pulling away. I can feel your indecision. And I'm trying to understand, but it isn't easy. If your powers are unleashed, it might be more years than I care to imagine before I could see you again." He turned to her. "Don't you see? If that happens, I won't have a choice. I'll have to let you go."

She leaned into him. Why did everything have to be so hard? She only now realized a part of her wondered if unbinding her magic might be the key to the kind of power and independence she'd always longed for. But it wouldn't be, would it? She'd be in more danger than ever, forced to live as a prisoner in the fae's realm.

She put one hand under the stuffed wolf, the other hand on top of Linc's, and held the animal with him. "Then I don't want it. I've lived without magic for all this time. I don't need it. There. Done. We don't have to worry about breaking the laws. I'm human. You're a wolf. We can have our baby in peace."

"It's not that easy. If you don't have your magic unbound, you won't be able to visit your father. You'll never get to know your people."

What would it mean to have magic? It was hard to make a life-changing decision when she didn't understand what it meant. But the idea of being away from Linc… Taking his baby from him would be cruel. Not to mention that she'd be as bad her mom, keeping her child from his father.

There was no winning, but her instincts pulled her toward this man who had captured her heart. And it had nothing to do with hormones.

Hell, she'd fallen hard. Whether he'd ever want her that way or not, she couldn't betray him. He might not ever love her, but he would love his child. He already did.

Bennett shook her head. "My people? My *people* are in this room. You, our son, and me. But you're right about my father. I need to figure out this thing with him on my own."

Linc closed his eyes and squeezed her tighter. "I understand. It kills me, but I do. I don't want to lose you. But I want you to have all the facts and see what you're giving up."

"All the facts?" She had no idea what he meant by that, but she leaned into him. God, he felt so strong.

"Your father is very powerful. Before you make any decisions, you should let him show you what you might someday be capable of. A demonstration of sorts."

She let go of the stuffed wolf, and he gently placed it back into the bassinet, as carefully as if it was their child. "I need to do this, whether I want to or not. Don't I?"

"Aye, lass. Because I know the one thing you want more than anything is family. You can't turn your back on him because he said the wrong thing. I value your loyalty, but I wouldn't be a decent man if I didn't tell you it's important to have family who will always have your back. I'm not sure I trust him. I'm not sure if you should, either. But you should hear him out. I believe he might have been a bit nervous."

Nervous? As if. The man was a king. "He wasn't nervous."

"Trust me, I would have loved to make him leave, but it isn't the right thing. So let's give him another chance, aye?"

He said he didn't want to lose her. She should be focused on her father, but all she could think about were those words. He didn't want to lose her, and he would do anything to keep her.

"Okay, but I swear to God, if he tries to pull the father card, I'm going to physically toss him out of this apartment myself."

He smiled. "And I'd pay to see it."

• • •

Idiot. Linc should have shoved the bastard out and been done with it. Now they were in the living room talking and laughing. Damn it. Why did he have to be so fucking honorable?

"Linc?" Bennett stood in the doorway to his office. In her knit dress and tights, with long boots and growing baby bump, she was gorgeous.

"Everything okay?" he asked.

"Yes. He wants to take me to the gardens. To, uh, show me what you were talking about."

Linc bit back a scowl. *Me and my big mouth.* "That's fine. Give me ten minutes, and I'll have the car waiting downstairs. Is there anywhere particular?"

"He says he needs gardens or forest. We could drive out of town a bit, but…do you think the Dallas Arboretum will work?"

The Arboretum would more than work—it was perfect. Quiet, contained. "That sounds like a good plan. I can have men on every entrance."

She shook her head. "Linc. No. Not men on every entrance."

"At least let me bring Nick."

"Okay. But just you and Nick—"

She flinched and grabbed her belly.

He jumped up and guided her to the sofa in his office. "What is it, love?"

"I don't know. I felt a twinge." She gasped. "Oh! There

it is again."

"Are you in pain?"

"No. It's…" She put his hand on her stomach. A small kick tapped against his palm.

Linc grinned, awestruck. He'd felt the small flutters before, but now his son was reaching out to him. "He's kicking."

"Yes, he is. Owww." She laughed. "Hey, little dude, that's my rib."

Linc chuckled. "You're so tiny, he's probably trying to find a way to stretch."

"God. This makes it all feel so real."

"I was thinking the same thing. He's really in there."

She scrunched up her nose adorably. "We made a baby, Linc."

"That we did, love," he whispered against her lips before kissing her.

She sank into him, her arms around his neck as her tongue teased his mouth. He pulled her onto his lap, and his hands slid under her dress.

Would he ever get enough of her?

No.

She was *it*.

His heart pounded as her grip tightened. Heat flushed his face. Bennett shifted on his lap, and his cock strained against his pants. He needed more. It wasn't enough just to kiss her—he wanted to *feel* her. She shivered.

"Linc?"

He pulled away and inhaled deeply, trying to calm his racing heart. "Love?"

"My father is in the other room waiting on us."

And that was a splash of cold water. Leaning his

forehead against hers, he whispered, "We'll finish this later."

She gave him a wicked grin. "Oh, we will and then some."

His cock tightened. He kissed her on the lips once more. "I'll be out in a few minutes. Let me get the arrangements made." And maybe take a quick cold shower.

Once she left, he picked up his phone and called Nick. After he told him what was about to happen, Nick was quiet.

"Do you think he's planning something?"

"I don't know. He seems to care about her, but it could be an act. I don't get the sense he would do anything to harm her. And kidnapping would cause her and the baby a lot of stress. Still, I don't think we can be too careful. I want the place as secure as possible."

"Trust me, brother, I have your back."

Linc hoped so. He hoped it wouldn't come to it, but he was willing to kill the King of the Fae if it meant keeping Bennett safe.

Chapter Sixteen

March in Dallas usually meant weather in the high seventies, but a cold front had come through and made it closer to forty. Not the best weather for walking through the gardens, but the flowers didn't know it was wintry. The place was one giant bloom and smelled like heaven.

Bennett's nerves were getting the best of her again. Her stomach churned in nauseating waves, and she picked at her fingernails with damp, clammy hands. She'd never seen magic. Not like her father had been talking about.

Calm down.

"Nick suggested we go to the Red Maple Rill area," she said to her father. "There's a stream and waterfalls, and it has a combination of trees and gardens."

"That will do nicely," he said. He'd seemed edgy in the limo. Though, with Nick and Linc staring him down, it was no wonder. She didn't exactly feel sorry for him. She'd in-sisted Linc back off with his suggestion to send a squad of security men with her, but to be honest, she appreciated her protectors. That didn't mean she couldn't see why it might make her father nervous. King or not.

And that was something she could *not* wrap her mind around. If her father was a king…then she was a princess.

"There's an area close to the small waterfall that might work best," Linc added.

She wasn't sure how he had made it happen, but they had the park to themselves for the next hour. Linc couldn't stop touching her. Every few minutes he'd kiss her head, or her cheek.

Something had changed in his office at the house. Their kiss had been explosive, and the way he looked at her—she couldn't define it.

Did he want something more permanent?

And why did she hope so very much that he did? They'd been clear from the beginning that they were just going to raise their kid together. But he kept looking at her in a way that made her think maybe he wanted more.

But she didn't want to go there. Not now. She had to get through whatever this was with her father. Then she could focus on Linc.

"This is the perfect place," her father said. They stood at the edge of the small creek leading down from the waterfall.

Linc took her hand in his. "It's all right, love," he whispered. "I'm here with you."

It was as if he willed his incredible strength into her blood. She squeezed his hand in response, and he gave her the most devastating smile. Really. That thing was dangerous. Fluttering craziness launched in her lower regions.

Focus.

Her father turned to her. "Would you like to see our home?"

"Maybe someday, but—"

"You misunderstand. It's not necessary for us to go anywhere for me to give you a glimpse of what awaits you."

"Okay…"

Her father lifted his hands, and before her eyes, the entire place changed. The stream and waterfall were gone, and in their place was a lush meadow. The gray skies disappeared, and the sun shone down. The air warmed and somehow seemed fresher.

"This is the meadow outside of my home," her father said. He waved his hand and their surroundings changed again. This time a castle straight out of a movie was before them. The stone structure was at least a city block long and had more spires than she could count.

"This is my home, Alororhha Castle. It has stood for more than a thousand years in this very spot, protected by some of the strongest magic in any world."

Bennett gasped. "How am I seeing this?"

"Illusion," Linc said softly. "A powerful one."

"So it's not really there?"

With a swipe of her father's hand, they were back in the Arboretum.

"You changed the weather," she said.

"No, I created my world in your mind," her father said.

"In all of our minds," Nick said from behind them. "You shouldn't have been able to break through my barriers. The most powerful of witches aren't able to do that."

His voice was edgy. Whatever had just happened, he didn't approve. And from the enraged look on Linc's face, he wasn't so happy either.

"So what else can you do?" Bennett tried her best to act like she wasn't that impressed, even though she was scared shitless. "Any Vegas magician can create an illusion."

Her father smiled. He opened his fist and hundreds of blue butterflies unfolded from his palm and fluttered around her. Blue Morphos, to be exact. She'd been fascinated by the creatures' iridescent sapphire and cerulean wings since she was a child.

"If you like that," her father said, "then behold."

A flock of blue jays flew around them and formed a replica of her face before dispersing.

Holy shit.

"There is more," he said. "Some things I cannot show you in front of others. They are well-guarded secrets, but should you decide to come home to your palace in Alororhha, I will show you the many wonders of our magic. Bound in you is a combination of your mother's magic and mine. She was every bit as powerful as I was back then, which would make you incredibly gifted. Maybe more than anyone we've ever known."

She snorted. No fucking way.

"I appreciate you showing me this," she said, her voice way steadier than she felt. "But why can't Linc just come with me, or visit at least? I don't understand."

Her father and Linc stared at each other.

"It's not that simple," her father said.

"Well, make it that simple—"

Linc shook his head. "He's not forbidding me to go. The magic there would kill me."

"And once we unbind your powers, it may take you

many years to learn to control them. You wouldn't be able to leave," her father added. "You and the child would need to stay close."

Bennett rubbed her forehead. "But my kid is half wolf. Won't the magic hurt him, as well?"

"He carries your blood and your magic, so he will be protected." He glanced at Linc, like he was issuing a warning. "You need to come home, Bennett. It's the only place you and the child will be safe. The wolf can tell you no different. Even if the Council allows your union, there will be those who will always be after you. But back in our realm, with me and your kind, you'll be safe."

He reached for her, but she backed away. Away from everyone. "Safe from what?"

"From the company of wolves and vampires," her father bit out.

And there it was.

She crossed her arms. "Those wolves and vampires are my friends and family. I'm not running off to some place I've never been with some guy who thinks he can tell me what to do. If you thought this power display of yours was going to win me over, you couldn't be more wrong. If anything, you've proven exactly the opposite. I'm not leaving the people I care most about. As far as I'm concerned, you can go to hell."

Her father growled, but to his credit — though little good it did him now — he softened his tone. "My daughter, I meant no offense — "

"Just stop." Everything from the past few weeks seemed to come crashing down on her at once. Her head ached, and her body trembled. "Linc, I need to go home. Now."

They walked away together.

Once they were out of hearing distance of her father, Linc said, "Just say the word, and I'll have every wolf in the area tear him apart."

"What do you mean every wolf in the area?" She looked around, and only now did she see the high numbers of security coming out of hiding from behind trees, bushes, hell, everywhere a person could hide.

"Just you and Nick?" She pulled away from him. "Isn't that what you said?"

Linc put up his hands in supplication. "You had to know I couldn't take that chance."

"The last thing I need right now is for you to be an over-protective asshole."

"Think about this," he said. "If your father's intentions hadn't been honorable. If he had tried something—"

"Then we'd have a fight neither of us wants," her father said.

They both turned and saw him walking toward them.

"What do you want?" Bennett said.

"I was worried I'd triggered something within you. Unbound you in some way." He shook his head. "Please know, the last thing I would wish you is any kind of harm. I only wish to protect."

"That disease seems to be going around."

She hated how he flinched, but she couldn't curb the anger in her voice.

"You did overreach. But it's just a killer headache. Probably a combo of North Texas allergies and not eating breakfast. Sorry guys. I didn't mean to worry you."

"I still think it best we get her home," Linc said in a

clipped tone.

"I've already called Jacinda," Nick added. "She's going to meet us there. Just to make sure you're all right."

"Fine," she said. "Fine. Oh my, God, my life has taken a weird turn. I'm hanging out with wolves, vampires, witches, and fae. I don't even know what half of *you* are." She waved a hand toward the security team. "Right now, I need a warm bath, a chicken fried steak, and some mashed potatoes. And pie. The baby really wants some chocolate pie. This kid has a thing for chocolate."

"And you'll have it," Linc said. He guided her toward the car.

"Your majesty," Nick said. "Why don't you come with my wife and I? There are some things I'd like to discuss with you." His tone brooked no argument.

Her father started to speak but then stopped. He simply came forward took Bennett's hands in his. "Are you well, darling girl? Please understand, it was not my wish to cause you harm in any way."

Bennett's head hurt like a mother, but she was fine. His concern seemed genuine, but she wasn't going to give him an easy out. He didn't deserve it. "I'm fine."

He frowned. "Really?"

"Really. It's just the last few weeks have been full of all kinds of crazy. It wasn't your magic. It was just everything. Plus, the pregnancy hormones, which just intensify all of it. I think."

He touched the top of her head, and the pain receded— even the wooziness disappeared. Was healing another of his powers?

"We'll talk later," he whispered.

"Maybe. But only if you stop with the bossy crap. I mean it. If you want me to trust you, don't try to pull me away from what's most important to me. Understood?"

"Understood. Get some rest, darling daughter." He followed Nick to the other limo.

She got into the limo with Linc and, finally alone, relaxed into the seat. "I can't figure out if he's a good guy or a bad guy," she said honestly. "He hasn't done anything that would make me suspect him of being evil, but he's a little too good to be true."

Linc glanced back at her father's car. "It's wise to be wary. Sometimes people *are* too good to be true."

"You're the one who told me to give him a chance."

"Had I a clue as to how much magic he holds, I would have been kicking his arse out the door hours ago. Beings with that much power, who have lived as long as he has…"

"What?"

He looked out the car window. "I don't know, love. I get no sense he wants to harm you or the babe, but I'm not sure how he feels about the rest of us."

"You think he'd try to hurt you?"

Linc shrugged. "I think if he wants something, he'll do most anything to get it. Men like him are always planning and plotting. He's managed to stay in power for hundreds of years for a reason. He's smooth, but Nick's on it. You don't need to worry. He won't try anything, not while we have you so well protected. And I think we have his adoration of you working for us. He doesn't want to upset you."

Bennett had done her best to set her father straight. And the man had seemed apologetic, but…she didn't trust him.

Because Linc was right. Sometimes a person *was* too

good to be true. She wasn't going to write him off. Not right then. But she wasn't going to drop her guard, either.

"Love, can I ask you something?"

She sighed. "If it's some big decision I need to make, it will have to wait. I'm done for the day."

"Nothing like that. You said that you don't want to leave the people you care most about. Did that include me?" His voice was low, almost a whisper.

Did he really have no idea how she felt about him?

"Yes. I do care for you, Linc." She was still too afraid to admit more than that. Let him take it how he wanted. If they got out of this okay, there would be plenty of time to figure out what they meant to each other.

He had tried to give her father the benefit of the doubt, even though she could tell it was the last thing he wanted. Should she do the same for Linc?

Should she trust the father of her child?

God, she wanted to, but it was tough.

She'd been alone for so long, and she couldn't just forget why that had worked so well for her.

He'd said he cared about her.

Maybe.

He took her hand in his and squeezed.

"Thank you."

She wasn't sure what for, but at the moment, she was too tired to think about it any further.

For now, she'd trust him to see her through what was about to come.

For now.

Chapter Seventeen

While Bennett rested, Linc went up to his studio. The gardens had inspired him to make some changes to a pair of jeans he'd been designing. He wanted embroidered flowers down the seam and one each on the pockets.

He would call them the Bennetts.

His cell buzzed and Marina's photo popped up. He didn't want to talk to anyone, but she'd keep calling if he didn't answer.

"Lincy darling. Can I come for my fitting today? I need to fly to Morocco for a last minute shoot. I won't be back until next week."

Crap. He'd forgotten about getting things together for the book. He'd been so consumed by Bennett and the baby that he'd actually neglected his work.

When had that happened? His work had been everything to him.

Bennett would probably sleep for a couple of hours, and

he really did need to get the fittings done.

"Sure. Come on in. I didn't know you were in town."

"Great," Marina said. "There was a shoot yesterday for Neiman's Christmas catalog. I'll be there in about ten minutes."

Which, in Marina's world, was at least an hour. That was fine. It would give him time to put the designs together and stitch up the prototypes. Usually, he'd have someone from his team come in and do it, but he was faster than all of them put together. And he could use the busy work to keep his mind off the morning's events.

He shouldn't have been happy that Bennett didn't seem that impressed by her father's powers. And she'd told him twice over her chicken fried steak that she was afraid something like that might be inside of her. Even if she could access that power, she didn't want it.

Thank God for the smallest of favors. If her father had thought to woo her to his side, he'd done the opposite. She was confused, which would give Linc time to plead his case. Twice he'd wanted to tell her how much he loved her, but both times he'd reminded himself why he had to keep those feelings to himself.

He needed to keep his distance so that he could be the protector she needed. Which meant he couldn't tell her how he felt. He wouldn't protect her body only to injure her heart.

He found the thread and fabric he needed and started working on the top Marina would be wearing in the photo shoot.

An hour later, his phone buzzed. The doorman wanted to know if it was okay for the model to come up. He already regretted agreeing to the meeting, but he couldn't avoid work forever. And to be honest, he needed to escape back into its familiar comfort.

"Lincy," she said as she came inside, air-kissing his cheeks. "Ready for me?"

The double entendre wasn't lost on him, but he wouldn't encourage her by acknowledging it.

"Yes, let's get you fitted." He turned toward his workroom.

"No time for a little play?" She reached out for his shoulder, but he pulled away.

A few months ago, he might have welcomed her touch and its momentary distraction. But now? There was only one woman's touch he craved. Scared the hell out of him, but there it was.

"Not anymore," he said. "I'm with someone."

She pursed her lip. "You're always with a special someone," she said.

Sometimes the truth hurt.

"Ouch. Guess I deserved that. This is different."

Marina shifted her hip to the side and crossed her arms. "How different is *different*?"

"I love her," Linc said.

Fuck. There they were, the three little words he'd denied. It felt good to say them out loud.

And to Marina's credit, it looked like she appreciated the significance of what he'd said, because she smiled and dropped any pretense of seduction.

"I must meet this woman who tamed the playboy's heart."

Hopefully, that'll never happen.

The last thing he wanted was Marina and Bennett comparing notes.

He just wanted the fitting over so he could get back

downstairs and tell her. Would she believe him? Shite. He'd need a plan. She would think it was about the baby.

He loved the child and had from the moment he'd heard about him. But he loved Bennett, too. Whether she was giving herself to him, or yelling at him with that wonderful attitude of hers, he loved her with all he was.

And he would protect the woman he loved. Her father? He would handle that now. Bennett would no longer be caught in the middle.

In the workroom, Marina started stripping, but he paid her nudity no mind. He no longer saw naked bodies. They were forms to which he fit his clothes. Not that he didn't appreciate women—he always would. But there was only one woman who could tighten his cock with a glance.

Nick was right. Linc had fallen for Bennett long ago.

"Ouch," Marina said.

Crap, he'd stuck a pin in her.

"Sorry about that. Here, slip it off. It just needs a few adjustments. You can get dressed and go."

He was already in the other room when he realized "needs a few adjustments" was just an excuse for a moment to take out his phone in private and bring up a photo of Bennett.

She'd worked her way into him so fully, so completely he was no longer in control of himself.

He wanted to call her and share what he was experiencing for her, but he couldn't tell her the depth of his feelings yet without blowing up the situation into something neither of them could handle.

Hell, it was a big enough problem that he was having these feelings in the first place. He couldn't keep her safe if he didn't keep his emotions in check.

This was bad. Really bad.

But there was a bigger problem than his emotions. Bennett's father. He was the person Linc needed to call. He was the person who needed to know how much Linc felt for Bennett and what he would do to protect her.

The phone rang only once before her father picked up.

"Wolf," he said. Just the one word.

"Fae King." Linc paused. "Let's settle this. Once and for all."

. . .

Bennett cricked her neck and stepped back from the painting she'd been working on. She pursed her lips. Maybe it needed some tweaks on a few of the animals, but it was a good start.

She was using canvas to work on the style she wanted to use for the mural in the baby's nursery. She'd taken parts of the gardens they walked through earlier and done some sketches. And then she created some tiny animals. Sweet little things, so far from her regular artwork, it was crazy.

But edgy, which was what she was known for, didn't really work in the beautiful nursery Linc had created for their son.

She sighed and set down the paintbrush.

The day had been too much of everything. The way Linc and her father had argued, she'd had half a mind to tell them both to shove their overprotective asses out the door and out of her life. But she couldn't say good-bye to her father, not when she'd just met him.

And Linc? He deserved the chance to be a father to

their child. But she wasn't sure she could be around him and be just friends.

Stupid me. Why do I always fall for the wrong guy?

She stepped away from the painting. Her art was the one thing that could soothe her, but it wasn't working.

"Knock, knock." Casey walked in, her arms full of packages. She'd rung earlier and said she was coming down.

"What is all of that?"

"Presents. I was really worried about you, so I made Nick take me shopping after we dropped off your dad."

"Presents?"

"For you and the baby."

"Oh." Bennett smiled as she took a few of the smaller bags from her friend. "Thanks. All of this is for the baby?"

They sat down in the living room. Bennett had the forethought to perch on the edge of a leather chair. She was a messy painter, and there was no telling what might be on her clothing.

"And you. Do you have anything for the nursery? I bought some stuff, but it's mostly clothes. Did I tell you Nick made me play twenty questions to find out the sex of the baby? Why didn't you tell me?"

"I just assumed you knew. Everyone else seemed to. You could have just called me."

"Yeah, but getting it out of Nick was way more fun." Casey waggled her eyebrows.

Pushing herself with her arms, no easy feat with her increasingly large belly, Bennett stood and motioned toward the nursery. "Come here, I want to show you something."

They stepped into the small room together, and Bennett bit her lip as Casey looked over the nursery.

"Oh, my God," Casey breathed. "This is beautiful. You guys did such a great job. I want to live in here. It's magical."

"Not us. Linc. He did everything. And he didn't buy the bedding, he made it."

Casey's hand went to her chest. "That's so fucking sweet."

"Hey, no cussing in front of the kid," Bennett admonished.

Her friend gave her the eyebrow.

"I know. I'm not exactly a saint. But I'm working on it. Yes, it was so sweet. I ugly cried in front of him. How's that for a thank you?"

"Awww. He probably secretly loved that you adored it so much." She set the packages down. "Some of these are for the baby, but I also bought you some maternity clothes." She gave Bennett the once-over. "Which you are so not touching until you get cleaned up. What have you been doing?"

"Working on ideas for a mural to go behind the bed. I'll show you in a minute."

"Oh, yes! It's going to look perfect there—I can't wait. Okay, so it's a boy. He's going to need some of these." She pulled out some cute little onesies. "I got like six different sizes because we don't have any idea how big he's going to be when he comes out. Nick said sometimes supernaturals can be a little bigger than humans."

Bennett cringed. That video from the Lamaze class flashed through her mind. Ouch.

"Yeah, don't remind me. Oh, I forgot to tell you about Lamaze. I wanted you to be there in the delivery room with Linc, in case he freaks out. But maybe you could just watch some of the videos online. I'm not going to lie, you may re-think the kid thing if you do."

Casey smiled. "I wanted to know what to do, so I already

watched two of them online as soon as you said you were pregs. I couldn't finish it. All the screaming and pushing. I'll be there for you, but it's good to have Linc. He may be the one picking me up off the floor."

They laughed so hard that they had to hold each other up until they calmed down.

"And I bought a ton of outfits." Casey held up the tiniest tuxedo Bennett had ever seen. "Nick insisted we buy a Cowboy's uniform, a Dallas Stars jersey, and this cute little Ranger's outfit. Oh, and I forgot about these little shorts and top from the Mavericks. And I thought maybe this could be his coming home from the hospital outfit."

It was a tiny pair of jeans and retro concert T-shirt. There was also a cute little pair of red Converse. It was something Bennett might wear, if they made the outfit her size.

"Oh—my—God." Bennett held the Converse sneakers up. "Where did you find these? They're perfect!"

"I know, right? Where's Linc? I bet he'd get a kick out of this."

Bennett put down the shoes and took a deep breath. "Before we go see him…I have something I want to tell you. But I need you to keep a secret."

Casey's eyebrows waggled. "You know I'm the queen of secrets."

"No. No, you aren't. You can't keep a secret to save your life."

"That's not true. I never told anyone about you dating David."

"God, don't remind me." He'd been one of their clients, which was strictly forbidden at the office. They'd done an ad campaign for his beer company. He was the perfect guy.

Took her to all the best clubs and restaurants. The sex was great. Not Linc fantastic, but pretty good. They'd dated for almost a month, and then one night he'd invited her back to his apartment. Where he was holding an orgy. She was pretty open-minded about sex, but she'd taken one look at the scantily clad group and turned and run way.

Casey was laughing. "I can honestly say when you showed up on my doorstep with ice cream, 'David invited me to an orgy,' was pretty much the last thing I expected to hear."

They giggled so long Bennett's ribs hurt.

"So this secret?" Casey urged.

"I think...maybe...uh..."

"You love Linc?"

Bennett did a double-take. "WTF. How did you know?" She leaned back on her hands. "I just figured it out."

"You two can't keep your eyes off of one another. It's been pretty obvious from the beginning. I think you two are the only ones who haven't figured it out."

So maybe she wasn't imagining his feelings. He might really care about her. "It scares me."

Casey leaned over and put a hand on her knee. "But he's a really good guy. And I've only known him a couple of months, but he's never looked at any woman the way he does you. I give him a hard time about the man whore thing. But he really doesn't sleep with them. Or not much. There was one about six months ago, but it didn't last long."

"How do you know about it?" She and Linc hadn't had a normal kind of relationship where they talked about past loves. Hell, she didn't like sharing that shit. And she had a feeling he wasn't much better about sharing his past than she was.

"Nick told me," Casey said. "We were talking about you on the way over. He was saying Linc has it bad for you. They've been friends for more than a hundred years and he hasn't seen Linc this serious about anyone. And I see that brain of yours working. He loves that baby, but he also loves you."

"Do you think?"

Casey raised her eyebrows, smirked, and nodded. "Oh. Yeah. I was watching him when we were at the gardens with your dad. He never once took his eyes off of you. And when you weren't feeling well, his face... God, he was so scared. I've never seen him like that. Nick's right. He has it bad."

Bennett grabbed one of the stuffed toy planes from the chair behind her. Did he love her? She would never know unless she asked him. More, she had to know if he could love her as a partner, not someone who would control her life in the name of protecting her.

One way or another, they had to figure it out.

"Can you hang out for a while? Let me get cleaned up, and then I'll see if I can find Linc. I wanted to show him the idea for the mural."

Casey frowned. "You might have to wait a while. I saw your dad heading up to see him as I was coming down. And boy, he did *not* look happy."

Crap.

Bennett's hands tightened into fists. She'd asked them to leave each other alone and let her deal with the situation with her dad herself, but what had Linc done instead? Exactly what she'd been afraid he would do. He'd taken her choice away from her to handle this the way he saw fit.

"Might be time for me to go kick some butt," she said. "I'm tired of people trying to make decisions without me and for me."

Casey cringed. "I'm really glad I'm not Linc right now."

Bennett narrowed her eyes. "You should be."

Ten minutes later, she walked off the elevator. Linc's raised voice vibrated the walls. She rushed—well, at that point, waddled—toward the office door and used the key card he had given her.

"You'll be dead before you even get close to her," Linc said. "You want her to see her home? She *is* home. And if you think I'm going to let you take her from me, you'll find out—"

Bennett came around the corner. "He'll find out what?" She didn't bother curbing her tone. The jerk deserved it. "Threatening my father? Really? Because that's helpful."

Her father grunted and walked toward the door. He paused by Bennett and said, "If this doesn't convince you about him, I don't know what will."

"Just go," she said. "Please. I'll meet you at your place later and we'll…try to figure this out."

Her father looked like he had a lot more to say, but to his credit, he simply shook his head and left.

When she turned back to Linc, he had a strained expression on his face. "Are you okay?" he said and took a step toward her, but she held out a hand to stop him.

"I told you this was my decision," she said. "I may be carrying your kid, but my brain and my body are mine. I will decide what I want to do. You have no say. Do you hear me? None."

"Take a breath. I'm just trying to protect you and your baby. You have no idea what that man can do."

He just didn't get it. Probably never would.

"That *man* is my father. He's blood. *You* are some guy who knocked me up." Linc flinched. Served him right. Asshole. "You don't get to make my choices for me. Ever."

She turned and made a beeline for the elevator.

She wanted to kill him. Of all the stupid, idiotic—he had no right to interfere with her life like that. Things were strained enough with her father, and he'd all but proven that wolves were temperamental beasts beyond control.

"Bennett, wait. You don't understand. Your father is dangerous. He might—"

She turned, backing into the elevator. "Might what?"

"Not might. He *does* want to take you home with him. Away from me." That last part came out as a whisper.

"Linc, do you care about me?"

"Of course I do. You're the mother of my son. Why do you think I've done all of this? Why do you think I brought your father here to settle this?"

And there it was. He cared for her. But in the end, he was like every other man she'd tried to love and be loved by. His idea of caring for her was to make decisions for her, all for her own good.

Another headache pierced her right eye. "We're done." She wasn't even sure what she meant by those words, but she had to get away from him.

Why did she have to have the feels for this guy? She didn't doubt he would be a good father. But she couldn't be with him as his mate, not when that would mean sacrificing the very boundaries that kept her safe.

He started forward, but she raised her hand to keep him at bay until the doors slid shut.

She held off the tears until the elevator started to move, but then she collapsed against the wall and sobbed. The universe had provided the slap in the face she needed.

The baby fluttered inside her.

"You have me, little dude," she said. "You will always have me."

Perhaps she finally understood why her mother had left her father, because right then, running away didn't sound like such a bad idea.

Chapter Eighteen

"What in the hell happened?" Casey screamed at Linc as she entered his apartment.

"Not what. *Who*. Her father," he said, the words coming out angrier than he intended.

He closed his eyes and pinched the bridge of his nose, breathing deeply. Dammit. He was *not* going to lose her because he'd lost his temper.

He opened his eyes and softened his voice. "Her father said she'd have to come back to the fae kingdom. What was I supposed to do? Just let him take her?"

"Well, no. But you can't fight her battles for her. That's exactly what she doesn't want." Casey frowned. "Listen, I know you want to go running after her. But she called me and specifically said to keep you away until she calmed down."

"Bullshit. She's going to listen to me."

Casey put a hand on his shoulder. "You stepped over

the line with the dad business. She's kind of independent. Maybe you've noticed."

At the time, it had seemed like the right thing to do to jump between her and her father. How could it have gone so wrong? So very fucking wrong.

"I can't lose her," he murmured. "You're her friend. Help me understand."

Casey put her hands together and cracked her knuckles, like she was getting ready to do some serious work. "Listen, here's the deal. She'll kill me for saying this, but she's fallen for you. She's been my friend for years, and I've never seen her in love. Ever. But do you know why she's afraid of being in love? Because every time she's tried to be with someone, they crowd her. Suffocate her. Try to do the man thing and control her life and make decisions for her. All for her own good." She cocked an eyebrow. "Getting a sense of déjà vu?"

Jesus. Some protector he'd turned out to be. He'd become her worst nightmare. No wonder she'd run.

Of course he'd fucked it all to hell. If he'd been smart, he would have given her the space she needed. He would have told her that he'd loved her from the first moment he'd laid eyes on her. He would have trusted her to take care of herself. He would have promised to be her partner in whatever way she needed.

That was what he'd been missing in all of his previous relationships. *Of course* he would eventually fail a woman who needed him to take care of everything. But a woman like Bennett? A woman who was fiercely independent? That was a woman who could offer him a true partnership.

"I love her, too," he said. "There's no other woman, and there's never going to be another one. She's it."

"I'm glad to hear it. But you have a tough road ahead of you. After the crap you pulled today, all you did was confirm her fears. It's going to take something big to convince her not just that you love her, but that you're the man she needs. Do you understand?"

He ran a hand through his hair. "I'll do whatever it takes. She's my love. My life."

She patted his shoulder. "That, my friend, is why you'll win in the end. You want some advice? This thing with her dad—stay the fuck out of it. Seriously. You have to give her some space."

Space? It went against almost every instinct in his body. But the strongest instinct, the one to love her in the way she needed to be loved, would always win.

He had to show her she could trust him again.

"Yep. You have your work cut out for you," Casey said, as if she could read his thoughts. "So what's your big play?"

He ran a hand through his hair.

"No fucking clue."

Chapter Nineteen

Bennett sat across from her father in the living room of his Grand Presidential suite at the Crescent hotel. There was a fireplace. In a hotel room. This man was used to luxuries she hadn't even been able to imagine. The place reminded her of Casey and Nick's penthouse — comfortable and super classy at the same time.

The shock on her father's face when she'd knocked on his door had been priceless.

She'd taken off her boots and then quietly sat cross-legged on the sofa. Her dad was sitting on the other end.

Nick and a few bodyguards were outside by her request. She was furious at Linc, but she wasn't stupid. She'd called Nick to find out where her father was staying, and when he'd offered to come with her and bring a couple of security guys, she'd said yes. As long as they agreed to stay outside the room.

"Do you think there will ever be a day when we have

privacy?" her father asked, smiling softly.

"That's part of why I'm here. I need to know your end-game." She was tired of pretending. One of her life mottos was to always put her cards on the table.

"I'm not sure what you mean."

"Yes, you do. You just found out about me. The father of my baby is a wolf." One she could never actually be with, but she couldn't think about that right now. "I can't live in your world unless my powers are unbound, and I have no intention of doing that. Ever. So what is your endgame?"

Her father had a worried look. "I did frighten you today."

"No. I mean, it was overwhelming, but it wasn't scary. What was scary was afterward. Something you said, and I think it's the reason Mom bound my powers and ran away."

He leaned forward. "Tell me."

On the ride over, it had come to her in one of those weird light bulb moments. "You said with you and mom's heritage that I'd have some whopping wild powers. I don't think she wanted that for me. You kept saying she was never comfort-able with being royalty, and she didn't care for the politics. But having a child, one of two of the most powerful fae…"

Her father frowned and sat back against the arm of the sofa. "You might be on to something."

"It was an extreme reaction, but being pregnant, I could understand. I wouldn't want my child to be the center of all that. Look at England and all the pressure put on the royal family, and then add magic to that. I think Mom made the only choice she could. And you were king, so she couldn't ask you to run away with her. She loved you, I realize that now. She never said a bad thing about you. Only that you didn't exist in our world. I didn't know the truth. Just that you were gone."

Her father flinched. He glanced away, and for a long time he stared at the painting over the fireplace.

"I never married," he said finally. "I've loved her for over twenty-five years. I'd hoped that someday she might come home." His voice caught on the word *home*. "Where she would have been safe."

Bennett didn't miss the implications of his words. He truly believed that she and her baby would be safer if they went back to the fae kingdom with him.

She understood his fear. He'd found his family, but now he was in danger of losing them again. And, though he hid it well, he was in mourning. The woman he'd loved for a quarter of a century had been taken from him by cancer, and the daughter he'd never known he'd had was pregnant with the child of the fae's enemies.

They were a mess. Like father, like daughter.

"At the end, before the cancer took her, she talked about the faeries," Bennett said. "The amazing parties they threw, and how she missed her faery king. I thought it was the morphine talking."

Her father raked a hand over his face. "If she hadn't bound her powers, she wouldn't have contracted the disease. I just don't understand why she wouldn't save herself. Why she wouldn't come back to me for help. You were grown. She didn't have to protect you anymore."

"I wish I had answers, but I don't." She couldn't stand it. Despite everything they'd argued about, he was still her father, and he was in pain. She slid down the couch and hugged him.

At first, his arms stayed by his sides, but then they

wrapped around her. "If she'd come to me and told me, I would have helped her. It would have killed me for her to go, but I would have done anything to please her."

She released him and sat back enough to look him in the eye. "And how long before you'd have gone in search for her? In some ways, I'm just like her. I understand why she didn't want to take that chance."

Her father stood and walked to the other side of the room, shaking his head. "It was my duty to keep her safe. As it is my duty to keep you safe, my daughter. I know you don't want to hear this, but your mate…"

"His name's Linc. And he's a good man." She paused, tasting those words. An overprotective jerk, but he was a good man. Her son deserved to know him. "More like you than you realize."

"But he's a wolf. That puts you in danger. I can protect you in our homeland, but I can't do that with you out here. It isn't safe. Even if we change the treaties, there are too many on both sides who think the old way is best."

She sighed and sat back on her feet. "I don't know if you guys realize it or not, but this is segregation. And telling someone who they can or cannot love is just wrong."

He started toward her, and she rose to meet him. If this was going to turn into a fight, she'd show him what he should have accepted all along. She could take care of herself, and she wasn't going anywhere she didn't want to go.

"Back away or I'll call the vampire."

Her father took a step back. "Okay," he said.

"You and Linc will have to figure something out. I'm telling you, he will be a part of my baby's life. Period. Understood?" She pointed her finger at him. No more pushy dudes.

Her father held his hands up in surrender. "Yes. I won't lose you again."

That was more like it.

Now, how would she deal with her wolf?

Linc crumpled up another sheet of paper and threw it into the trash bin. He'd tried writing letter after letter to explain to Bennett why he was sorry, how he loved her, why she should trust him again, but they all felt wrong.

Because in the end, what would a letter do to convince her she could trust him again? A letter was just words, and he'd ruined enough by saying the wrong ones.

Maybe it was finally time to admit he didn't have a clue what he was supposed to do next. Maybe it was time to admit even a lone wolf sometimes needed help.

He brought out his cell and dialed Nick's number.

"Casey tells me you've gotten yourself into a fucking mess," Nick said.

"Yeah," Linc said. "Now that we've established I'm an asshole, could you do your friendly duty and get up here and help me figure out how to fix this?"

Nick laughed. "Casey wants to know if she can come, too."

"If Casey can help me win Bennett back, she can come over anytime she wants."

Linc hung up and began pacing across the room, but then his cell rang again. He picked it up without looking at the caller, ready to tell Nick to stop messing around and get down there—

"Linc." The voice was but a whisper.

"Bennett?"

"Something's wrong," she whispered, the pain evident in her voice. "Please. I need you."

Linc was up and out the door. He didn't dare wait on the elevator. He'd take the stairs.

Nick and Casey were coming out of the elevator as he opened the door to the stairwell.

"Linc," Nick said. "What the hell are you—"

"Call 911," he yelled as he ran into the stairwell. "It's Bennett!"

He ran down the stairs with the phone to his ear. "Are you in the apartment?"

"My bathroom. It hurts so bad. So bad…" Her voice fell off into a pained moan.

His heart was in his throat. "It's going to be okay. Breathe for me, love. Remember. Pant to help with the pain."

"Too soon…"

She was right. It was way too early for her to be in labor.

This was his fault. The fight he'd had with her father, then the foolish words he'd said that had driven her away from him. The stress of the day had been too much.

Please, God. Let her be okay. Please.

His hand was shaking so bad he could barely get the key card in the door. He ran for the bathroom and found her curled up on the floor.

"Love," he said as he scooped her up into his arms.

"Not getting better," she groaned. "It's supposed to stop."

He put his hand on her belly. It was tight and harder than usual. "Breathe. Come on, lass. Take a deep breath."

"Can't."

"Look at me, dammit." He pulled her chin up. "Open your eyes." She did. "Breathe with me." He did the panting thing they'd learned in the class. After a few seconds, she followed him. He let go of her chin and put his hands on her belly. The muscles were loosening ever so slightly.

Tears formed in her eyes.

Dammit, he'd be following her down that road if he didn't take control.

"No, love, none of that. He's just a bit early. We can do this. I need you to be strong for all of us. I promise I'm more scared than you could ever be right now. Shaking all the way to my bum."

She gave him a weak smile.

"Now, deep breaths. In and out, nice and slow."

Casey skated into the bathroom, nearly slamming into them.

"Jesus, what is it about you two and all the running?" She put her hands on her thighs while she tried to catch her breath. "Nick's on the phone with Jacinda. She's three blocks away. She'll get here before the ambulance, which is also on the way. They need to know if she's having contractions and how far apart they are."

"That was the first," Bennett said hoarsely. "I thought they were supposed to be mild and work their way up. This fucking hurts."

"Okay." Casey pulled out her phone. "I'm going to time them. So the last one just stopped. We wait for the next one and see how far apart they are."

"Fuck no," Bennett said. "I can't do it again. Tell Jacinda to get here and give me some fucking drugs. Now. Oh, shit."

"Two minutes apart," Casey yelled out to Nick.

Linc grabbed her chin again and pulled her focus to him. "Breathe." He panted with her. Sweat had formed on her brow. The pain had to be intense. Too much, too fast.

"Love. You look in my eyes. We're doing this. You and me. Got it?"

"Fucking bossy," she groaned.

She had him there. But in this, if nothing else, he couldn't make her choices for her even if he wanted to. He couldn't give birth to the baby for her, but he could be there for her as the man who loved her, and as her partner.

He shook his head at his own foolishness. This was what she'd wanted all along. He'd just been too blind to see it.

"Oh, fuck!" she screamed.

"Jacinda's here," Nick yelled from somewhere. "EMT's are downstairs."

Jacinda rounded the corner and very nearly ran over Casey.

"Get her tights off," she barked to Casey.

"Hey, you," Jacinda said to Bennett. "Stop freaking out. You're thinking it's too soon. It is early, but from the sonogram, we know his lungs are in good shape. And that's the main thing that we're really worried about at this stage."

"Hurts," Bennett said.

"Do something," Linc told Jacinda. "Give her something to make it stop. It's too hard too fast."

"Okay, Dad, listen to me good." Jacinda pointed a finger in his face. "She gets to yell and say whatever she wants. You need to stay calm, or I'll kick your ass out. Got it?"

That made Casey and, more importantly, Bennett, laugh.

"Yes, ma'am."

And he had to admit that with the doctor there, a calm had settled over their little group. It was going to be okay. Jacinda was there. This was normal. Early, but the baby and his love would have their best chance.

Bennett giggled. "You said, ma'am. Ouch. Ouch. Don't make me laugh. Ouch."

"So, straighten up, Bennett. Labor sucks," Jacinda warned. "You're going to hate us all by the end, until you hold your son in your arms. That's your end goal. Get that baby out safely. That's all we're trying to do. Casey, you may want to step out for a second and get us a blanket or two. I need to check a few things."

After taking her blood pressure, Jacinda waited for the next contraction and then stuck her hand up Bennett's dress. "Okay, we're at a seven. That gives us some time to get to the hospital. Linc, you want to follow behind?"

As much as he wanted to be right there by Bennett's side, he was ready to follow behind if that was what she wanted.

But she said, "No, he comes with me. He's my coach. I need him." She glanced up at him. "Don't leave me. Don't ever leave me."

"Never, love. I'm here. Always. I love you. I will always love you."

"Casey told me I should give you another chance. But— trusting is hard for me, Linc."

"I know, love. We'll sort it all out. We will."

She closed her eyes as another contraction hit. "Motherf—"

Everything moved so fast after that, Linc felt he was in the middle of a whirlwind.

They were having a baby.

Chapter Twenty

The birthing room at the hospital was supposed to be calming. It looked like a hotel room, but there was nothing soothing about any of this. "Shit, it hurts!" Bennett screamed at Linc. "This is your fault, you stupid asshole with your stupid super sperm. Knocking me up when I wasn't ready."

Her vow to stop swearing had gone right out the door with the first contraction. And if he weren't supernatural she'd be breaking the bones in his hand.

"I'm sorry, love."

"No, you aren't." She groaned. "I fucking hate you."

He suppressed a grin. God, he loved her. And somehow, someway, he would convince her that he was worthy of her.

"I know you do," he said.

"Stop patronizing me with your sexy voice and charming ways, you Irish fucking asshole. How am I supposed to resist that?"

Jacinda smiled at him from behind her facemask. He

couldn't blame her. Bennett was hilarious. Maybe someday he'd tell her about it.

"I'm going to have to edit a lot of this video if you keep talking like that," Casey said from behind the camera. "Your poor child will be traumatized."

"What is wrong with you people?" Bennett snapped. "I'm giving birth here. Until you pull a child out of your crotch, you show some respect. Got it?"

Casey choked back a laugh, and Bennett glared. "You're supposed to be my best friend. You should be strangling this asshole for doing this to me."

"Okay. Take a deep breath," Jacinda said calmly from between Bennett's legs. "Two more big pushes, and you'll have your baby in your arms."

"Thank *God* you are here," Bennett said to Jacinda. "You're the only sane person in this room."

After taking a deep breath, Bennett squeezed her eyes and groaned loudly.

She was in pain, and there was little Linc could do. Bennett gripped his hand tightly, but it had to be a tenth of what she was feeling. He used his free hand to push her hair back from her face.

"You're a brave one, love. You can do this."

She puffed again and pushed. And as she did, she stared at him as if she were drawing strength from him. He held her eyes, trying to show her how much he loved her, that he was there for her, and that together, they were strong enough to make it through anything.

The babe's cry tore their attention from one another.

"Well, much like his mother, he has a set of lungs on him," Jacinda said.

"We did it." Bennett collapsed back on the bed.

"You did it," Linc said, beaming at his tiny son as the nurses cleaned him up and swaddled him.

His son. Joy clogged his throat, and his chest tightened with love. In a heartbeat, his love for his little family was all encompassing. He couldn't breathe. Tears burned his eyes.

Casey and Bennett were sobbing. He turned to smile at them, and that's when he noticed Bennett's face.

"Love, are you feeling all right?"

"I just had a baby, moron. I'm kind of tired." The nurse put the child in her arms. She touched the babe's cheek lightly. "I'm so glad you're here. That's your daddy. He's not as scary as he looks. And that's your auntie Casey. She's going to spoil you rotten." A flash of pain crossed her face. "Um, ow. I thought the hard part was over. My head hurts really…" Then her eyes fluttered closed.

"Jacinda?" Linc said.

The doctor frowned. "Her pressure's high." She checked Bennett's vital signs and gasped, and the exposed emotion, so raw it couldn't be hidden, made Linc terrified. "Nurse," she said. "Get them out. Now!"

In a rush, a nurse lifted the baby out of Bennett's arms. Her face had paled even more, and her breathing was shallow.

"What the hell is going on?" Linc demanded.

"Get out," Jacinda ordered. "I need a CT scan stat, and get the neurologist. Not Cawley. Call Branson. He was upstairs prepping for surgery. Move, people. Move."

The bed was wheeled out of the room before he could process what was happening. He looked from his son to Casey, who was bawling.

"I'll stay with the baby," Casey said. "Go. Go find out

what's happening." She waved him away.

He glanced one more time at the babe as if to assure himself his son was fine.

"His Apgar score is great," the nurse said. "Go, be with your wife."

Linc ran down the hall just in time to see the elevators close. "What floor?" he yelled at the woman at the desk.

"They're taking her to four, but they won't let you in."

Like hell they wouldn't. He raced up the stairs, grateful for his supernatural speed.

The team had paused just outside one of the surgical units. He raced to grab Bennett's hand. She was so cold, where she'd been so warm before.

"Love, can you hear me?"

"She's out," Jacinda said. "Her pressure is really high. We've given her meds, but she's not out of the woods yet."

"What is it?"

Jacinda shook her head. "We don't know. I just checked her eyes. Possible stroke. Has she had headaches? Dizziness?"

"Yes to both," he said. "But isn't that normal?"

"Yes, but not in this case. We're scanning her, and if she needs surgery I've got the best man for the job ready to take her on. But time is of the essence. I can't stand here and explain it to you."

"Save her. Do you understand me? She is my reason for breathing. Save her."

Jacinda put a hand on his arm. "I'm doing my best."

"Should I call a mage?" He knew he should have called one of the healers to be on hand for something like this. Dammit.

"That's why I called for Branson. He's one of the best

neurological surgeons in the world, *and* he's a healer. He's her best chance. But we've got to go now."

Linc let go of Bennett's hand, and they wheeled the woman who owned his heart away.

"Let's go." Nick's arm wrapped around his shoulders. Linc hadn't noticed him following him up the stairs. "Come on. Let's check on your son. I talked to the nurses. They'll call us soon as they know something."

"I don't want to leave her." Linc's voice was a whisper. Numb with fear, he wanted to crawl onto the gurney with her. Hold her until he knew she was all right.

"You aren't leaving her. She's getting the best care possible. But that baby needs you right now. You don't want his first moments to be staring at strangers. He should at least be able to look at your ugly mug."

"The baby…" Linc's mind was a fog.

You must always protect our son. He comes first.

Her words tore at him.

Bennett was dying.

He hit his knees.

"Hell." Nick knelt beside him. "Look, she's going to make it. Let's take care of your son. They've got him cleaned up. Casey just texted me. She hasn't let him out of her sight. I'm supposed to bring you down to the nursery. I know it's hard right now, but you need to be there for your kid. He's counting on you."

That's right. He had to be there for his son. He wouldn't be like his father.

"And they'll call about Bennett? I can see her as soon as she's out of surgery? In recovery?" He glanced up to find his friend frowning.

"Yes. Jacinda or Branson will call as soon as they know something. They won't let you down, and there aren't two people in the world who are better at this sort of thing."

Linc followed Nick down the hall, a hollow feeling in his gut. What should have been the happiest moment in his life had gone horribly, horribly wrong.

She hadn't been strong enough to carry their child.

She was going to die alone in that room, and it was his fault.

He'd never forgive himself.

Chapter Twenty-One

Bennett tried to open her eyes, but the light was too bright.

"Nick, turn out the lights," Linc ordered. "They're causing her pain."

Wow. Mr. Bossy was back. Ordering everyone around. She tried to think what had happened, but her brain hurt. The baby.

"Where's the baby?"

"He's fine. Nick's holding him right now. Open your eyes and you can hold him yourself."

She squinted, but it took her a bit to focus. Just as she saw Linc, the nurse came in the room and pushed him away. Jacinda and another guy followed the nurse.

"What's with all the drama?" Damn her throat hurt. "Why are you guys staring at me?" she croaked. "What happened?" She glanced around the room. It was a regular hospital room, not…

Wait. Hadn't she been in the birthing room? How had

she gotten here?

"You scared the hell out of us," Jacinda said. "Nurse, give her some water."

The nurse held a straw to her lips, and the cool water slid down her throat. She sighed a breath of relief. That was *so* much better.

"Why didn't you tell us you've had headaches the last few weeks?" Jacinda asked, and it wasn't in her usually friendly tone.

Bennett frowned. "Jesus. What's with the third degree? Did I pass out and hit my head? I can't remember."

"Your blood pressure went through the roof, and you passed out," the guy who'd come with Jacinda said.

Holy hell.

"I'm Dr. Carlin Branson, a neurologist. Look at the light, please." She followed his light. "Now, my finger." She followed it.

"The headaches?" Bennett asked.

Jacinda crossed her arms over her chest. "You should have told us. Linc said you'd been having them off and on. It's a sign of preeclampsia. "

"I'd read that women get headaches all the time in the last trimester, because of changes in hormones," Bennett said. "I didn't want drugs for them, so I didn't see any sense in complaining."

"They weren't hormonal," Dr. Branson said. "Your pressure must have been high off and on. You could have had a stroke." He held up his hand as she opened her mouth. "You *didn't*, but you could have. You'll have to take it easy for a few months."

"Jesus. Can nothing ever go right for me?"

"Well, you did a pretty good job with this guy." Linc placed their son in her arms and beamed at her.

"Is it just me, or does he have my mouth and hair? Though the rest is all you." She put a gentle finger in her son's tiny hand. "He's perfect." Her eyes watered. Stupid hormones.

"That he is." Linc stared down at their son with loving eyes. She couldn't blame him. He was the most adorable baby ever.

It hit her. Shit. "God, I would have been the worst of mothers if I'd died."

"Was never going to happen." Linc said it as if it were a forgone conclusion. "I wouldn't have allowed it."

"If you could have been saved on sheer will alone, Linc would have done it," Casey said. "He refused to believe you wouldn't wake up."

"Yeah, he was a right pain in the, uh…" Branson began, but then seemed to remember he had his professional reputation to uphold. "But he loves you, so that's expected."

Branson was right about that. She could see in the way Linc looked at her, and the way he held their son, that yes, he loved her. But there was also something different in his eyes. Something that made her now feel safe and secure.

Casey reached down and kissed her cheek. "Nick and I are going to run and get some stuff for the baby. We'll be back in an hour. Do you want anything?"

"A cheeseburger, sweet potato fries, and a giant chocolate milkshake."

Everyone laughed.

"Well, my love hasn't lost her appetite. I'm glad to hear it," Linc said.

My love. Those kind of words had always made her worry what would come next, how the relationship would inevitably fall apart, but the way he said them, she'd give anything just to hear them again.

"Is it okay?" Nick asked the doctors.

"She can have whatever she wants to eat," Branson said. "And I read in the chart that you wanted to breast feed, but we had to put you on some medication. It would be best for now to give the baby formula."

God, she was lucky to be alive. Too surreal. She glanced down at the little version of Linc in her arms.

Heart in throat, she sniffed. Her baby. He snuggled deeper into her chest, and she lost her heart for good.

"The nurse will take your vitals every few hours," said Jacinda. "We'll have to keep an eye on you for a few more days. The baby can stay with you in the room. If you need help, you need only push the button."

So much to remember. So much going on. She held the baby a little tighter to her, unable to tear her eyes away from her child. "I…uh…"

"I'll be here," Linc said. "I'll take care of her and the babe. Do you want to feed him?" he said to Bennett. "It's about time for his two-hour feeding."

"You do need someone with you at all times to help with the baby," Jacinda said. "Right now, we don't want you lifting him too much. He's a hefty eight pounds. But you can hold him as much as you want. Just make sure you have a pillow for support."

Bennett nodded.

"Now, on a scale of one to ten, what's your pain level right now?" Jacinda asked.

"My head, probably about a six. My body, a twelve. I feel like I was hit by a truck."

Jacinda smiled. "That's a fair assessment. Labor is tough on you, but you'll bounce back quickly. The nurse will be in later to tell you things to look out for with aches and pains. As far as your head, if you have a sudden onset of sharp pain, or if that pain inches toward a seven or eight, tell us immediately."

"Okay."

"We'll give you some time alone," Jacinda said. "If you need anything push the button. Don't tough it out."

"Get some rest," Dr. Branson said, and then he followed everyone else but Linc out and shut the door.

"Don't ever do that again," Linc whispered.

"What?" The fog in her brain was slowly lifting. She stared down at her perfect baby. "He's healthy, right?"

Linc touched her cheek. "Yes. He's as healthy as he can be. And you..." He paused and swallowed, and she saw again that flash of emotion in his eyes that made her feel safe and secure. Like she was home.

Something was different about him...

"Linc," she said. "What do you want to say?"

He took her hand in his. "I'll do whatever you want. Abide any wish you want to make. You can go with your father if you must, but please don't ever run away from me again. I can't stand the idea of being in a world where you don't exist." He kissed her forehead. "I love you more than my own life. I would have given my life for yours if I could have."

"Are you having sympathy hormones or something? I'm sorry I scared you, but I'll be fine. You don't have to make all these crazy declarations."

"Bloody hell, woman. I love you. I think I have from the moment I met you."

"Don't cuss in front of the baby."

He chuckled. "I meant what I said. I do love you. And I know now what that means. I'll respect your wishes from now on. If you wish to take the babe…" His voice broke. "If you wish to go with your father… That's your choice." He cleared his throat. "I won't stop you. I love you, Bennett, and I'm here to support you no matter what you choose."

If she hadn't been sure about her love for him, she was now.

Was it possible to be this happy?

"I'm a woman of my word." She forced herself to frown. It wasn't easy with the joy clogging her throat.

"I know that," he said solemnly. "I understand why you need to go."

"Dude. *So* not going anywhere. I told you that. I won't take your son away from you. I have no idea what the future holds or how we're going to do this, but I want us to do it together. I love you, you dumb jerk."

The biggest grin broke across his face. "You do?"

"Well… You better give me a kiss, just so I can be sure."

She grabbed his shirt before he could respond, and then she brought him close.

Damn, the man could kiss.

She pulled back and looked at the ceiling, as if considering it, then said, "Yeah. I'm pretty sure… I do. I love you. Probably loved you from the first time I met you. But don't let that go to your head."

"Never," he said. And then he kissed her. Careful not to smush the baby, he showed her everything that was in his heart, and she gave it right back to him.

When they finished, he grabbed a tissue from the side table and dabbed her cheeks.

"Hormones," she said gruffly.

He took a deep breath. "I want thou to be my wife. For all eternity, I want thee bound with me. I will be ever faithful and protect thee with my life. This is mine oath of fidelity to thee. I am thine. Thy partner in everything. Thy life mate."

"Holy hell. Eternal oath? That sounds like a big deal."

He brought her hand to his chest. "I've never made this oath before. I've never wanted to. But with you? I love you. I love your stubbornness and loud mouth. I love your kindness and your heart of gold. I even love your decorating skills. My home will never be the same, and I'm the better for it."

Tears welled and spilled onto her cheeks. He loved her. "Moron. You're making me cry."

"The babe can hear you." He dabbed her eyes with a tissue. "You have to stop with the swearing and calling me names. I don't want him to grow up with a—what is it Casey says?—a potty mouth."

"I'll take it under consideration."

He brought his face close to hers. "I'll spend the rest of my life doing my best to make you happy," he whispered against her lips. "Do you accept my oath?"

"I love you, uh, you big hunk of an Irishman. And yes, I accept your oath. I pledge my love to you. I don't have a fancy oath, but I'm yours."

He chuckled, deep and rumbling. She loved that sound.

Her heart was so full of love for this man and their child. And she was grateful to be alive. More so than she ever had been before. She would appreciate each and every day with them.

She cocked an eyebrow at him. "So partner… Life mate… Maybe now would be a good time for you to start on your fatherly duties and get me the baby's bottle."

"Yes, my love."

• • •

"Bennett?" Her father rushed through the door to her hospital room and to her side. "They told me you almost died."

Linc rose with the babe in his arms. He didn't want her father upsetting her. One look from Bennett and he backed off. She wanted her father to meet their son. Fine. But this was tough.

And that was enough to quell Linc's anxiety. No matter what happened, he and Bennett would face it together.

"Shhhh," Bennett said. "Your grandson is sleeping." She pointed to Linc, who held their son in his arms. "I decided to have some blood pressure drama at the worst possible time, but I'm fine. And the whole death thing was an exaggeration. I just passed out for a bit."

Her father had a hold of her hands. "I was so worried when Nick called."

"She only woke up an hour or so ago," Linc said. He was standing on the opposite side of the bed from her father.

"Thank the goddess," her father said. "Did they say when I'd be able to take you and the baby home?"

Linc suppressed a growl in his throat. She was his. No one would be taking her anywhere.

Bennett rolled her eyes. "I can see you getting all puffy, Linc. Calm down. You've been so good this afternoon. Don't start now." She turned to her father. "Dad, I–uh… Linc, you tell him."

"We're getting married," Linc finished. "We love each other, and we don't care about the outdated treaties or anything else you might use to keep us apart. She is my beloved, and she will be for an eternity."

Bennett sighed. "What he meant to say before he got all cave man wolfy is that we love each other. And this baby, well, you should see his birth as a sign of peace, Pops. Linc's going to be my husband, and you're just going to have to nut up and get with the program."

Her father arched an eyebrow. "Nut up?"

"As in suck it up. Be the king and tell people how it's going to go down. I love him and he loves me, and I feel like I'm singing a fucking *Barney* song. Shit. I mean— Oh my Gawd, this not cussing thing is going to be hard."

Linc sighed. "Sir, I love her. I will protect her with my life. And we will protect our son with our lives. But the lass and the babe will be staying with me. Not because I will it, but because that is her choice."

Her father's eyes narrowed as he turned to Linc. "May I see the child?"

Bennett gave him the stink eye. "Before you touch him, you swear an oath that you won't do anything crazy. You won't walk through a magical mirror or turn into a dragon and fly away."

God, Linc loved her. She had no problem expressing feelings.

Her father stared at her like she was crazy. "I will not harm the child, nor ever dare to take him from you."

Then he glanced up at Linc as if to ask if she was

mentally stable.

Linc shrugged, then winked at Bennett.

"I'm not crazy," she said. "Just protective, something you two should understand." She smirked. "Okay, you can hold him. But I'm watching you."

Linc reluctantly passed the baby across the bed to his grandfather.

The other man chuckled. "He's heavy for one so new."

Linc took Bennett's hand in his.

Her father moved around the bed to sit in the recliner in the corner of the room.

"You'll make a strong warrior prince someday," her father said.

Bennett cleared her throat. "Dad?"

He smiled. "Just a phrase. And we are at peace, for now. But there may be a time when he will be expected to take the throne, and I will make sure, with your permission, that he is ready."

This time it was Bennett who sighed. "For now, can we just focus on everyone being alive and here? I don't know about you guys, and I'm not one who usually does this sort of thing, but I'm counting my blessings. I have a son." She sniffled.

Linc leaned down and kissed her forehead. "We have a son."

"And I have a grandchild." Her father smiled. "A fine boy, who will grow up to be as smart and fierce as his parents."

Bennett took his hands and squeezed.

"We have a family," she whispered reverently.

Not one for tears, Linc blinked his back.

"Aye, luv, we do."

Epilogue

The couple's baby shower was in full swing, but Linc only had eyes for his wife and child. He held baby Liam while Bennett opened presents, surrounded by friends, many of whom had become their family.

Linc was happier than he'd ever been in his life. Didn't matter that he was sleep deprived and living with a hormonal maniac whose moods changed from one second to the next. He welcomed it all. Gave her whatever she wanted, whenever she wanted it.

He was so grateful his lass was alive and well and giving him hell.

"What?" she mouthed when she found him looking at her.

"I love you," he said. Not bothering to whisper.

A blush spread across her cheeks. "I love you, too, doodle."

That was her nickname for him. They both knew it meant 'moron', but she'd cleaned up her mouth since they came home from the hospital. God, he loved her for it.

Everyone around them paused.

"So when are you two going to get married?" Casey asked, watching the pair of them.

Linc glanced at Nick.

"Actually, I was hoping we could borrow a certain Greek tycoon's island in a couple of months when my lass and babe are ready to travel."

"Say the word," Nick said as he patted his friend on the back. "It's yours."

"Oh, yeah. I forgot to tell you guys," Bennett said. "We're engaged." She held out her hand to show off the ring he'd given her at the hospital. Right after he'd said the second binding ritual, which was about five minutes after her father had left. Linc wasn't taking any more chances. As far as he was concerned, she was already his wife. But he would go through the traditional American ceremony to please her. Well, with Bennett it probably wouldn't be very traditional, but he didn't care.

His lass belonged to him heart and soul. Everything else was, as she liked to say, cake. For the rest of their lives, he would show her just how grateful he was to her for teaching him the meaning of love.

Acknowledgments

I want to thank everyone at Entangled for their help. It starts at the top, thank you Liz P. for believing in me. You are a wonderful human being who has done so much for authors. Stephen Morgan, you are one fine editor. Thanks for your patience and encouraging words. From the amazing marketing and publicity teams, to Curtis our managing editor, thanks. You guys are awesome. A quick shout out to my lovely agent Jill Marsal, who is gets my crazy. You are the best!

I want to thank Linc's fans, who loved him so much in "Take It Like a Vamp," and waited patiently for him to have his own book. I wrote this book for you guys. I hope you love Linc and Bennett as much as I do. You have no idea how much I appreciate your kind and encouraging words.

About the Author

Bestselling author Candace Havens has written multiple novels for Berkley, Entangled and Harlequin. Her books have received nominations for the RITA's, Holt Medallion and Write Touch Reader Awards. She is the author of the biography Joss Whedon: The Genius Behind Buffy and a contributor to several anthologies. She is also one of the nation's leading entertainment journalists and has interviewed countless celebrities including Tom Hanks, Nicolas Cage, Tom Cruise, George Clooney and many more. Her entertainment columns can be read in more than 600 newspapers across the country. Candace also runs a free online writing workshop for more than 2200 writers, and teaches comprehensive writing class. She does film reviews with the Hawkeye & Dorsey on 96.3, and is a former President of the Television Critics Association.

Discover the **Take it Like a Vamp** *series...*

TAKE IT LIKE A VAMP

Vampire Nick Christos might've been born in the Middle Ages, but the good old days seem tame compared to the last eight years he's spent ruling the Supernatural Council. His only respite is with his cute neighbor Casey Meyers, a woman he wants more than any undead man should. Now he'll risk everything to save the human he's come to love.

Also by Candace Havens

LIONS, TIGERS, AND SEXY BEARS, OH MY!

A RIVETING AFFAIR

TYCOON REUNION